UNDER A
BLACKTHORN BUSH

UNDER A
BLACKTHORN BUSH

JOHN CONNERY

Red Hill Publications

First published 2006

Published by Red Hill Publications
PO Box 557 Craigavon BT64 9AG

Copyright: John Connery

Printed by Nicholson and Bass Ltd, Belfast.

ISBN 0-9546142-1-6

Author: John Connery

Title: Under a Blackthorn Bush

Front Cover: *Under a Blackthorn Bush*, by John Connery

To my special daughter, Jill,
from whom I learn something about Life every day

If you're lucky enough to live till you're eighty, or ninety, or a hundred – or more – and you're able to take stock of your life up to that point, how much of it will you actually remember? Sadly, relatively little. All memories therefore – whether good or bad – are precious.

Rua Flynn

John Connery is a landscape painter from County Down, in Northern Ireland. His love of the Irish countryside and its people inspires both his painting and his writing.

His first collection of short stories, *The Insular People*, and now *Under a Blackthorn Bush* were written on days off from painting. They are drawn, needless to say, from the uniqueness of his fellow countrymen and women, and the breathtaking landscape in which they live.

CONTENTS

THE BURNING OF
KILMORE CASTLE

I'M TOLD THAT, IN COMPARISON WITH OTHER LANDLORDS and landed gentry, Lord Kilmore of Inniscurry was one of the more decent spuds. I didn't personally know any of the others – I was only a boy of five or six at the time – and I hardly ever set eyes on old Kilmore himself, so I can't confirm either way. But of what I heard all those years ago – around the kitchen fire of a Saturday night, or in the street as I impatiently held my mother's hand wishing she would quit the gossiping and come on home, by all accounts his Lordship never did anyone any harm. As they say, he would've done y' a good turn before he done y' a bad, and that's why I can't understand why there was any need to burn the old bugger out.

My father would have told yarns as we sat round the fire each evening as the smell of boiled spuds and cabbage hung in the air and bluebottles bumped and buzzed at the window. His own clothes harboured the smell of hay, musty baler twine and horses. He was a tenant farmer and wrought on Kilmore's estate, while my mother was employed on a part-time basis in the castle's laundry room.

Kilmore Castle sat at the top of Inniscurry's main street; the street that led to Belfast in the north and Dublin in the south. At one time, before a diversion was made away from the castle's main gate, part of the yew-lined stately walk from the front door of the castle to a little ornamental pond in the grounds was part of the main Belfast to

Dublin road, traversed by horse-drawn carriages, coaches and all manner of carts and drays.

The mansion seemed not to be of this world. It sat, unearthly, as if floating above the town, demanding respect and awe from the citizens; always there, but never really a part of the town. It was known only as the Big House, like every other mansion in Ireland. With its tended gardens, demesne wall, Pleasure Grounds, pond and lake the Big House was the unbidden centre of all that went on in Inniscurry. All you would hear in those days was the Big House this and the Big House that. Always the Big House. If the rents were raised for the tenant farmers it was never said, 'Lord Kilmore is putting the rents up.' No, what was said was, 'The Big House is putting the rents up.' You would have heard, 'There's a quare swanky do goin' on in the Big House the night', or 'So 'n' so's got a job at the Big House'.

The locals were glad of the employment the Big House brought. At a time whenever any type of work was hard to find in the country, and hundreds of families were uprooting and moving to the city for work in the shipyard or the factories, to be able to live and work in the fresh air was a welcome bonus. This wee country of ours has never been rich, except in beautiful scenery and kind, honest hearts, but the Glens of Antrim and the Giant's Causeway and all the goodwill in the world won't put spuds on the table. Old Kilmore employed fourteen servants, six of whom were from the town and surrounding townlands while the others had been brought over from England and Scotland, already trained as housekeepers, gamesmen and gardeners. There were three groundsmen. The head groundsman, I believe, was from Aberdeen, but fair play to the Big House, because Sean O'Rourke and Jimmy Conlon from the town were the other two. It had stirred some amusement in the town when Kilmore came along and employed Jimmy Conlon; up until then Jimmy's nickname had been the Poacher, for obvious reasons to everyone except, obviously, his new employer.

My mother and two young girls from the townland of Ballyvicnakelly – Geraldine Hegarty and Kate Gorman – had good paying jobs in the laundry. At that time Geraldine was more or less supporting her family, and her only sixteen. Her father had been ploughing one day but the leather reins, which had been draped over his shoulder, got snagged in the works and he was trailed over the plough, breaking his leg in two places and dislocating his hip. His recovery had been tediously slow, so the money from the Big House was particularly welcome.

I suppose Old Kilmore wanted to integrate into the local community to a degree which suited him, but he, and his ilk, never really managed it. To him, we – the Irish – were always *they*, never *we*.

Every once in a while we'd be playing at marbles or hoops in the street, or I'd be walking along with my father for a dander or whilst going visiting to some far off destination at the other side of the town, when we'd hear the rattle of saddlery and fresh horses trotting, and down the hill would come his Lordship, decked out with top hat, his trimmed pointed beard and waxed moustache barely moving as he chatted to his prim wife beside him in the carriage. He expected the locals to doff their caps at him – most of the men did, but it was more than usually done with begrudging hands and a bluffed deference; anything to keep the old snob content enough not to raise the rents. As soon as the carriage had passed Murray's barber shop at the corner, the men would replace their caps and roll their eyes skyward and say things like, 'The oul' eejit's lookin' well the day!' and, 'Was that his moustache, or was it his eyebrow down for a drink?' Or even, 'The missus is lookin' very glum this mornin' – she mustn't have got it last night,' and all the men would roar conspiratorially and then go back to their business as old Kilmore and the missus trotted off obliviously towards Belfast.

We always had a bit of a laugh when the hunting season came round. His Lordship was, admittedly, a very experienced horseman, and his young daughter, Anna, obviously took her way with horses from him. They say she was an accomplished rider by the time she was four, and as the years went by you'd see her out and about, always in full control of some fine spirited animal. Well, at hunting time some locals were lucky enough – depending on how you look at it – to be invited to join old Kilmore at the hunt, so, like boys in a classroom eager to please and impress their teacher, they accepted their invitations. The town's shopkeepers used their draught horses; horses that throughout the year were employed as clattering old nags, pulling barrels of beer and crates of milk, now found themselves jumping ditches and following hounds. The police Sergeant would come along, borrowing some farmer's mare and spending the day bouncing along in the saddle like a distressed dinghy in rough seas. The magistrate, Mister Cunningham and the town's inebriate doctor all joined in, desperate to impress, but spending more time in the sheuchs than on their horses.

On cold days my mother was tasked to be at the castle early to help get the huntsmen ready and would be the one who would supply their stirrup cup before they set off – a snobbish tradition, but my mother was happy enough to do it. My father used to castigate her and say she was going too far along the servitude road. He complained, often and loudly, but, like every Irishman, one thing he didn't complain about was the extra few shillings, or duck at Christmas which my mother was given as a thank you from the English invader. My mother, a feisty woman at times, would half-jokingly accuse her husband of taking money from Kilmore with one hand and stabbing him in the back with the other.

When his Lordship's daughter got married there was a huge affair in Inniscurry. The Kilmores supplied all the food and drink in a tent erected on the front lawn, and the music and dancing went on for two days. Some over-indulged, not having seen so much food and drink in all their lives, and a week later Joe McNabb from the town was found dead in the lake, probably having imagined in his drunken stupor that he could walk on water. Anna was married in the little Church of Ireland – which stood quaintly and choked with ivy within Kilmore's demesne – to some Lieutenant Colonel or other, and she no sooner had the ring on her finger until she was living the high life in England, while gallivanting all over the world with His Nibs.

That left only his Lordship and her Ladyship, trying to manage the country house by themselves, which became a daily struggle. One housemaid, Kate Gorman, was paid off and Geraldine Hegarty, the remaining maid, found herself helping the head butler and other lads to seal off entire wings through lack of use, and to save on fuel and light. Slowly but surely the power and the wealth and the influence was seeping away from Kilmore and his fellow landlords like water out of a bath. It seemed that the Kilmores didn't, or couldn't, observe the times and how the warp and weft of society was changing, and anybody with an eye in their head could have seen from a mile off that the jolly days of landlordism were as good as over in Ireland.

And then there was resentment, too. Resentment by most nationalist elements and all republicans that Kilmore and his cohorts had no right to be in Ireland in the first place. The Invader had crossed the Irish Sea once to claim Ireland as British, and then he claimed it again – forty thousand acres at a time – for the unlimited pleasure and high lifestyles of the English landed class. And by 1922 those certain militant elements – whose ranks and strength had swollen by popular opinion and who would pervade the island of Ireland for the next eighty years – had had enough of doffing their caps.

Coupled with the Land League, civil war and the Plan of Campaign, new power was handed to men who wanted English aristocracy out of Ireland once and for all. Some mansions and castles were burned to the ground in a blaze of unheard-of publicity. A number of landlords literally ran back to England, leaving their homes still smouldering, to face a new dilemma: up until then the Irish had looked upon them and treated them as English, and now the English in England viewed these returning exiles as Irish emigrants. They became nomadic refugees. Some landlords stayed their ground, asserting with vehemence that they would never be intimidated out of their homes.

On an autumn day Lord Kilmore received news that Moydrum Castle, belonging to his old friends Lord and Lady Castlemaine had been razed to the ground, and the couple were presently making arrangements to return to England, seeing no future in Ireland anymore. Kilmore was fearful, and feared for his and his wife's safety. Then Palmerstown House, and more friends – Lord and Lady Mayo – uprooted when their home and possessions went up in flames.

There are few things in my life that I remember as vividly as the night – well, it was really in the early morning – when our whole family was wakened by my father's excited shouts of, 'They're burnin' the Big House! They're burnin' the Big House!'

I could hear my mother's whispered admonishments to him that he'll waken the children, but we were already wakened and scurrying about trying to get our clothes on, while my father scrambled with his braces and boots, dancing to get his trousers on in a hurry while I leapt out of bed, my feet chilling instantly on the new oilcloth floor and raced to the scullery to find my mother dressed and – yes, typical woman – couldn't be seen in the town even in the middle of the night without combing her hair and putting on her lipstick.

The whole town was out. Gaunt, ghostly faces. It was a cloudy night and as we trotted up the main street towards the Big House the first thing we saw was the orange glow reflecting on the underbelly of the clouds. A mysterious, terrifying, once-in-a-lifetime sight. As we turned the corner at Houston's pub we were met with the growl of the conflagration, like a continuous deep wind, sucking and blowing and spitting and crackling. I thought that hell had visited us on earth.

Sparks and flames shot like bullets into the chilling night air as the Big House groaned and burned, clinging to life as its roofs plunged downward into the fire. The town's square was lit as if by daylight, windows reflecting the inferno, making it appear as if the interior of each dwelling was also alight.

There was a stunned hush amongst the townspeople. We could hear Kilmore's servants shouting orders at each other and trying to douse the flames, but with the occasional, half-full bucket of sloshed water it was futile. The horses, with eyes standing in their heads, were being released by the stable boys into the demesne at the back. I held my father's hand tightly and when I looked up I could see my mother crying into her handkerchief. It made me want to cry as well, but I didn't look up at my mother and so make things worse. My father saw her crying too and put his free arm round her shoulders. Some other women had their handkerchiefs to their eyes as well.

'For God's sake can we not help them?' my mother cried. Men were standing all around, uneasy, shaking their heads as good people desperately wanting to help a neighbour in distress but knowing that there were men in the crowd who called themselves volunteers who would see any form of aid as assistance to the enemy.

'We daren't,' I heard my father say quietly, 'too many eyes.'

We heard later that at about one in the morning about thirty armed men had arrived in the town wielding an array of weaponry, the result of a well-planned operation. They were dressed in ordinary clothes and most of them, according to witnesses, were barely twenty years of age. A couple of them marched theatrically across the square, through the gates, across the lawn and brazenly knocked on the front door. The rest of the militia surrounded the slumbering building, awaiting further orders. The front door wasn't opened to the intruders, but by this time the live-in servants and staff were rushing about, waking the Kilmores. When entrance continued to be refused, the order went round to smash the lower windows and enter.

A couple of the leaders made their way upstairs where they were met with the pyjama-clad Kilmores on the landing, looking dazed and bewildered. The old pair became frightened and one of the gang told them they had ten minutes to get as many personal belongings together and get out. Then he added in a clipped northern accent that they were burning the house as a reprisal for recent atrocities committed on nationalists by the Black and Tans.

As the Kilmores and their staff rushed about, gathering together trivial things like items of toiletry and photographs and some jewellery, the raiders entered each room and piled its furniture into the centre. The furniture included tables, chairs, cabinets, mats, paintings, tapestries. In the drawing room alone there were chintz-covered chairs, inlaid tables for chess and backgammon, and wool-worked stools. A cabinet full of rare china, blue-and-white plates, watercolours, oils, a piano and a harp were stacked like a mini bonfire, almost touching the chandelier, and then saturated with petrol and set alight. Some of the more dedicated members of staff still tried in vain to extinguish the flames, but were soon beaten back by the ravaging blaze.

As we pressed ours faces against the warm wrought iron gates of Kilmore Castle, gates crafted in the nearby town of Richill a hundred years previous, watching in tremulous awe the flames' yellow and orange tongues lick high up in the night sky, our glowing faces all agog at such a sight, we saw old Kilmore and his missus, silhouetted on the front lawn, defeated and helpless. He put his arm over her shoulders as his home, possessions, and life were incinerated in front of him. Jobs would be lost, dreams would be abruptly ended. Two horses, and Kilmore's wolfhound Ulysses, died in the blaze.

And all we could do was stand and watch in guilty silence.

UNDER A
BLACKTHORN BUSH

SHE ARRIVED IN TRAMORE with the clothes on her back, a small case of necessities and memories, two shillings which her mother and father had saved up for her, and a vague possibility of work at the country home of Mr and Mrs Shillington. She was sixteen, and even though the town of Tramore was only forty-two miles from her home in Inniscurry, it was strange and unfamiliar, its oddly shaped main street, new faces glancing at her over their shoulders, and a stifling smell of turf-smoke and sea air. She scanned the new shops that lined the one steep street: Charles O'Donnell – Meat Specialist & Undertaker. She smiled inwardly, if nervously.

This was the furthest Geraldine Hegarty had ever been from home, and the nagging fear crossed her mind that she may never see Inniscurry again. Even her father, a man who never spoke of his age but who must have been about forty, had never set foot outside his home town of Inniscurry in his life, except for once when he travelled by train to Dublin for his brother's funeral. He planned that trip for two weeks on hearing that Sean had died of the smallpox, and on his return he took to his bed and stayed there for three days; the experience had taken so much out of him.

Tightly she held the two worn and crumpled letters; one from her mother to her possible new employers, telling of Geraldine's industry, cleanliness and housemaid skills, and the other a recommendation from Lady Kilmore, her previous employer, who had been kind enough to send it all the way from England, returning there after the fire at her home in Inniscurry six month previous.

Geraldine was lucky. The Shillingtons of Tramore House were a housemaid short after the recent disposal of Pearl Hamilton. Pearl had wrought at Tramore's big house for twenty-four years; a good hard worker, but over that time had taken an awful fancy to the green dinner set, one of twenty-five such dinner sets used at the Big House for various functions. Over a ten-year period she managed to pilfer the entire set; a plate hidden up her skirt one evening, a cup concealed up her vest the next, a silver spoon secreted in her sock... Until one evening Mr Shillington was out hacking on his skittiest mare when the horse was spooked by a pheasant flapping out from a hedge and Mr Shillington went sprachling over the mare's head and swiftly broke his leg with a thunderous crack on impact with the road. He dragged himself to the nearest cabin in which he could see an oil lamp burning, to find it was the home of Pearl Hamilton, his loyal and faithful housemaid of twenty-four years, with his green dinner set all nicely laid out on the table for Mr and Mrs Hamilton and their six squabbling children.

Geraldine Hegarty settled in well and quickly, and within a few weeks, when she had a full grasp of all her duties she began to love the place and the new challenge in her life. Mr and Mrs Shillington were helpful and courteous, and as long as the work was done efficiently and on time, and no-one purloined the dinner sets, they were happy.

She loved the setting of Tramore House. It was set at the end of a long avenue lined with red cedars and giant oaks, and faced out to Donegal Bay. She got to walk into the town three mornings a week for fresh meat and bread, and soon knew all the shopkeepers and many of the townspeople by name. She was known as the black-haired lassie from Inniscurry.

She wrote home to her mother and father frequently, telling them in excited words how her wages were £15 a year, plus lodging, for a six-and-a-half-day week. She couldn't have earned that sort of money anywhere at home, she wrote, but although the hours were long – from 5.30 in the mornings to whenever she collapsed, exhausted into her bunk around ten each night – the air was fresh, the company was good and the meals fit for a queen. She lit all the fires first thing every morning, dusted and swept the big drawing-room, library, dining-room and two beautiful sitting rooms. Then the two housemaids met in the kitchen, had a quick cup of tea and biscuits themselves and then either Geraldine or Mrs McCord, the senior housemaid, would take Mr and Mrs Shillington their first cup of tea up to bed before preparation for the breakfast began in earnest.

Dinner parties were always sumptuous affairs; Geraldine loved to change from her daily black and white maids' uniform into the brown and cream one for special occasions. At such events, all maids and butlers worked together to ensure each function's success; they polished the silver until it gleamed, cleaned the glassware until it sparkled, and all the linen was newly washed so that it was spotless for the guests. The head butler – Xavier Quish, a ruddy faced, rotund wee man with an officious cough – saw to it that the maids got the remains of the best of the food, thanks to the guests usually being such picky eaters. Sometimes this meant whole slices of lamb, only delivered by the town butcher that morning. On Geraldine's first Christmas at Tramore House, she was astounded and touched to find that the Shillingtons had left presents for the staff in the maids' quarters on Christmas Eve.

'What way do you go into town when you're goin'?' asked Mrs McCord one morning.

'Along the main road, past the hotel, and on past the police station. Why?' Geraldine replied, darning a sock. The morning sun was bursting through the tall windows, making the white linen on the table gleam.

'There's a shortcut y'know. Sometimes it can be mucky if it's been raining, but on a dry day it's a lovely walk.' Geraldine put down her needle and yarn and questioned Mrs McCord with her raised eyebrows. 'Turn left as you go out the gate,' Mrs McCord went on, 'then over Hungry Hill. Follow the wee loanin' over the hill and when you come to a fork go right and there's a path down that takes you right to the back of O'Donnell's the butcher on Quay Road.'

'Oh,' said Geraldine, eager to try the new route next time she was going to town; maybe the next day.

'You're not superstitious, are y'?' Mrs McCord added in an inquisitive, playful way, smiling and folding some neatly ironed handkerchiefs.

'No… not really… why?' Geraldine asked.

'It's just that there's a big blackthorn bush – more like a tree – at the side of the lane just past Hungry Hill. There's a derelict house beside it… the Boyles used to live there. Some say the fairies won't let you past without bad luck befalling you, and others will tell you the bush has brought them good luck. Oh, I don't know, I'm not superstitious – I think it's just a lot a oul' men sittin' round a fire for want of somethin' to talk about – and I've been walkin' past it these ten years and it hasn't done me or mine any harm.' It was a long speech for the usually taciturn senior housemaid. 'You can't miss it. Look out for it the first time you're passing. Many's a time I've stood under it for shelter, and boys, it doesn't half keep y' dry!' she laughed.

Geraldine had no fear of the blackthorn bush, or tree, or whatever it was. The only person she not so much feared but tried to avoid when possible was the town idiot they called Hector. As Hector passed in the street, herding his one old cow wherever he went for no reason, tapping it on the rump with a stick, the boys and girls would sit on the window sills and shout 'Hek! Hek! Hek! Hector!', and toss an occasional lump of turf in his direction when his back was turned. Hector, unaware of the taunts, would wave the ash stick and shout back, 'Mornin'! Fine mornin'!' His tufted unkempt hair stuck up at the front and resembled the flea-ridden fur of a dead dog, while his only pair of trousers barely made it below his knees. Parents in the town used Hector as a lesson in personal hygiene, but not in any complimentary way. It was told that at one time Hector was a happy, very intelligent boy who had aspirations of becoming a doctor, and according to all accounts this was a realistic ambition. He had one bad habit, however, and that was his morbid addiction to picking his nose. Pick. Pick. Pick... at every opportunity when he thought no-one was watching. He would relish the hauling of a greenhorn from his nostril, twiddling it between his fingers until it took on the solidity and elasticity of plasticine, and then would delight in flicking his product at something and trying to hear it land. Sometimes, if it wasn't the correct consistency, he would stick it behind his ear and work at it later when he got the chance. One day, however, when the young nose-picking Hector's forefinger was buried deep up his right nostril, and he was blindly engrossed in the effort, (legend has it) a friend came up behind him and, accidentally but with quite a force, shoved Hector's elbow, forcing his finger right up into the base of his brain, causing irreparable damage. Since then, in the town of Tramore, and even to this day, when a parent catches their young boy picking his *willick*, they will scold and say you'll end up like Hector the Halfwit.

Geraldine's wild mountain-blown hair and gentle green eyes won many admirers, secret and not so secret, not least a certain Declan Quish, the eighteen-year-old son of the head butler, Xavier Quish. A gangly, uncouth youth, Declan was a farm labourer outside the town, but hoped someday to work for the Shillingtons. His straight sandy hair and pointed chin gave him a snipey appearance and, working long hours on a farm seemed to ensure that he was fated always to have some breed of animal's dung under his fingernails and blocking the pores of his hands. He was a pleasant enough chap with a kind smile, but somewhere in him lay a vicious streak, the sort that harboured no qualms about poking a stick through a frog, or dropping a cat down a well, or locking a dog in some forgotten outhouse until it starved to death.

Geraldine had been in a daydream as she ambled the shortcut to Tramore when she heard the slapping of boots behind her and turned to see Declan Quish jauntily jogging, almost bashfully, to catch up with her. He slowed to a walk, looking sideways at Geraldine. Up close he could see the dimples at the corners of her lips and his heart did somersaults.

'You're new, aren't y'?' he said when he got his breath.

'Not really; I've been working at the Big House for six months now,' Geraldine said, turning and continuing to walk on.

'I seen y' in town the odd time…'

'Then if you've been watching me, why did you ask if I was new?' she said, keeping her eyes firmly fixed on the rutted laneway in front, but a secret, wry smile curled the corners of her lips.

'You work for my da… did y' know *that* if you're so smart?'

'I didn't know Mr Shillington had a son your age… he certainly never mentioned you.'

'Not Mr Silly Shillington!' said Quish. 'Mr Quish; head butler.'

'Whatever in the name of goodness made you think I work for him?'

'He tells you what to do, doesn't he?'

'Indeed he doesn't! He shows me what to do if I need help, sometimes, but he doesn't tell me. Only Mr and Mrs Shillington tell me what to do. And by the way, his name isn't Silly, either.' Geraldine was supposed to be surprised, or impressed that this young man was the head butler's son. But she wasn't. In a small existence like Tramore everybody knew everybody else, and everybody's business and everybody's connections. But if the truth be told, she had caught sight of Declan in the street one market day haggling over the price of a pig and admired him from afar. She was secretly glad of the chat now, strolling along on this fine day, but as sure as shooting she wasn't going to let him know it.

For the next few weeks Declan tried to time his visits to the town so as to coincide with Geraldine's errands every Wednesday morning, and she got used to his footfall behind her, and him out of breath, always pretending, with a bashful crimson face that their meeting was a pleasant accident. He would chatter about work on the farm, in the fields, the accidents which invariably occur around machinery and horses. Geraldine talked of Inniscurry, how her father was, the letters she would write and the ones she received from home.

'That bush over there's supposed to be bad luck,' said Declan one day out of the blue, pointing to the blackthorn while pushing his fringe out of his eyes.

'I don't believe in all that,' said Geraldine, tutting. 'If you believe that something is bad luck, then it becomes bad luck… that's all.'

'You're a feisty one, all right,' he said. 'But I know that once a boyo from the town lifted a bird's nest out of that bush and when all the wee scaldies had their mouths open he cut their tongues out with a razor blade – just for pure badness. And y' know what? All his children were born with no tongues… none of them could ever speak.' Geraldine winced at the image, but cast the yarn off with a shrug. Declan believed it; his eyes were wide and excited. Maybe the boyo from the town – whoever he was – believed in the bad luck of the fairies, too. Anyway, Geraldine allowed Declan's hand to slip into hers as they passed the bush, and when they were safely past its ragged shadow he took it away and stuck both hands in his pockets.

One day they were able to stop for a minute – both had been early at their chores. They sat on a flat rock near the blackthorn bush and

Geraldine breathed in the sea air, squinting into the sun at the gulls swooping over the distant trawlers.

'Where do you think we come from?' she asked presently.

'Tramore,' said Declan.

'I don't mean that…' she said, and the boy put his hand over his mouth and sniggered impishly.

'I know what you mean! From your mammy's—'

'I don't mean that either. I know where babies come from. I mean… do we come from the stars, or the air, or the ground? I mean your soul.'

'I never give that much thought; we're just here because we're here.'

'Then what do y' think makes y' the person you are?'

'I don't know. Your parents, maybe. The church. Yourself,' he said, shrugging.

'I'd love to know what makes us all different… and yet the same. I'd love to know what gives us all our own identity; y'know, why do I look like m' mother, yet have m' daddy's hands? Why do you have the exact same cough as your father… and the same pointy nose?'

'Do I?' he said, and coughed as if to prove it. She laughed, throwing her head back. It was the same arrogant cough, as if chastising, but not really meaning it. He laughed as he ran his finger the length of his nose. 'Nobody ever told me I had m' da's nose before, but you're right – I have!'

They got up as Geraldine picked some bracken from her skirt.

'I'd like to marry you some day,' he said.

'We can't be talkin' about such things at our age,' she said, looking up quickly from her skirt.

'At our age? Sure some people are married at our age and have a family!' She laughed, her dimples piercing her cheeks, but Declan didn't like the tone, as if she were sniggering. There was a few seconds' pause then he said, pointing to a far hillside where sheep grazed, 'Look over there…' And while here eyes were distracted he reached out and grasped one of her budding breasts, squeezing it hard before she could escape. His clumsy grip was painful and she whimpered.

'See!' he said, aroused and proud, 'when I marry you we can do that all night in the bed!'

Geraldine strutted off, her face fuming, her mind confused, tears of pain and hurt in her eyes, wanting to shout back that he was the rudest, most uneducated person she had ever met in her life. But she gathered her shawl and said nothing. 'Come on back, Geraldine,' he shouted after her, 'Givvus another feel at your ditties!'

She didn't see him for weeks after that. He obviously made some excuse not to be in town on market days, nor was he seen standing at the corner with his mates in the evenings. Xavier Quish had hinted that his son never mentioned her now whereas at one time it was Geraldine Hegarty this and Geraldine Hegarty that, all day long. He must be busy, his father had forwarded, as he passed the laundry room, but Geraldine just folded the towels and the sheets and got on with her work.

The summer faded into the violet hues of autumn and the first sloes, like hard black bullets, appeared amid the green and yellow stippled leaves of the blackthorn. She found herself on the darkening lane on her way back to the house after having collected some apples and plums from the new greengrocer's in town, and wondering what had become of Declan Quish. She saw the outline of the bush looming in the fading light ahead. For the first time ever she felt apprehensive about passing, for what, she didn't know; just some intuition made her want to return to the town with her apples and plums and walk the long way round. It would take her another half hour, she thought, but Mrs McCord would be waiting for her now to help prepare the evening meal. A light drizzle had begun to fall, so light that it rested on her eyelashes.

She stuttered as the dark green shape grew up ahead, trying to tell herself to be realistic and remember how the blackthorn always looked so innocent and pretty during the day and why should everything change because the hills were growing dim. She thought of the man who cut the tongues from the nestlings and a chill ran up her spine. She walked on, dying to get past that bush, her heart now pounding in her ears and the sound of her feet on the gravel. As she passed she wanted to run but she was entranced and frightened. A cool breeze blew the drizzle into her eyes and the small leaves twittered. She couldn't help but stare, and suddenly there was a great weight on her back, forcing her to the ground in the direction of the bush, grunting, clinging to her, dragging her over the damp grassy bank and under the bush's branches where it was shadowy and cold. The man had his hand over her mouth and yet she tried to scream but it was like screaming in a nightmare; no sound, just a muffled moan came out. Her basket of apples and plums scattered over the laneway as she struggled to free herself but the man was too strong. She fought, trying to bite the palm of his hand, trying to kick his legs, but the lower she was pressed into the grass the less she could do, and he, the animal, knew it. She thrashed about, yelling inwardly, and managed to twist her head enough to come face to face with Declan Quish's ferret features, up close, breathing on her, half smiling. The determination in his eyes terrified her.

'There's nobody to hear you screamin'!' he threatened; a menacing tone, pulling her blouse and cardigan apart at the front and finishing what he had started weeks ago, grappling, squeezing. But even though his uninformed mind started out wanting only to fondle her young breasts again – God, he'd thought about nothing else for a month – now, as he rolled over on her, holding her down, with her struggling, a beastly, untamed urge took over and he wanted more. Geraldine's eyes widened like those of a frightened foal. She knew what he was wanting, and she was powerless to stop him.

In a gross entanglement of legs, arms, skirt, underskirt, trousers, trouser belt unbuckling, legs being forced apart, hoarse, breathing, sharp like an exhausted dog, wondering what will happen and if it will be painful, keeping her eyes closed, the moon came out from behind misty clouds.

And there was Declan Quish, standing over her, his hair wet and hanging over his eyes, sweating, panting, confused and awkwardly pulling up his trousers. He stared down at her lying there in the nettles like a broken doll, and in an instant he was running away, over the rocks and heather, stumbling and falling. Geraldine Hegarty managed to stand up, her exposed bloodied legs white in the moonlight, and braced herself against a bough of the blackthorn. With the last of her trembling energy she shouted after the disappearing figure, 'Curse on you, Declan Quish! Curse on you!'

HARRISON'S HAPPY HENS

ROBERT HARRISON'S FAMILY LEFT THEIR HOME on the west coast of Donegal when he was ten and ended up in Dublin's north side, where his father found work in the docks. Young Robert left school at seventeen with very few educational qualifications. He just hadn't been the academic type. He was a bright enough boy; the teachers liked him, he wasn't a bully, and, like all pupils who are neither tyrant nor genius, he was quickly forgotten.

Wandering from job to job for a while, working at anything that gave him some pocket money, he served in Martin's General Store on the Drumcondra Road and later checked eggs for damage and defects at the Derrylin egg plant at Lucan.

Before he turned twenty he secured the position as a clerk in an insurance company in Talbot Street. It was the sixties, and without photocopiers, faxes or printers, all correspondence had to be written out laboriously by hand. As a by-product of having to write everything down he learned the inner workings of things; by writing and remembering he understood how the cogs of industry and commerce worked, and by face-to-face communication with the public he learned to wheel and deal. He perfected his knowledge of quotations and premiums and by repetition day after day he could have quoted almost *verbatim* the complete laws and procedures in relation to any type of insurance. It was a profession that he had never even considered in his youth, but the more he learned the more he liked, and the more he liked, the more he learned.

Evening after evening he had no sooner finished his tea when he put on his coat and began plodding the dark, smoggy backstreets of the north side. Some doors were closed abruptly in his face, others opened to tense, snarled faces that had no more interest in insurance than a turkey on Christmas Eve. But one in fifty homeowners invited him in, one in ten made him a cup of tea, one in a hundred offered him a dram of whiskey for the cold night. And some signed up for a new policy, or additions to their existing ones. This is what he lived and worked for; he had found the perfect niche.

The thrill was in the sale. He learned that if a kind, cosy family allowed him entrance to their private domain, and if he got the opportunity to expound upon their insurance needs as he saw it, it was totally and utterly his own fault if he walked back out into the cold Dublin streets without a signature. He got used to spotting that moment of indecision, of doubt, when a wife didn't even want to consider the possibility of being left without her husband, never mind paying good hard-earned cash in waiting for that day. The husbands would be usually more pragmatic; one wit argued that life insurance is something that leaves you penniless while you're alive so that you can be rich when you're dead. There was that special moment when a husband didn't know whether to politely decline or sign up. It was like hooking a fish and then manoeuvering it into your net.

He did well. He perfected the hard sell – a term that hadn't as yet come into vogue – he advised well and put enormous energy into his work. But most of all Robert Harrison was honest. Honest about doing a day's work, honest with himself, honest with his customers. So much so that after two years he and his wife were able to move to fashionable Booterstown, into a house overlooking the sea. A year later he launched his own business – Harrison Life – and devoted more time – sometimes twenty hours a day – to his new venture.

His wife, Aisling, backed and supported him at every juncture.

They had two young children – a boy and a girl – but every spare minute at home was whiled away in tax returns, invoices, ledgers and receipts, making plans for future development.

At the beginning of the seventies an opportunity presented itself, and Harrison, with expert intuition and acumen grabbed it with both hands. Every evening the RTE six o'clock news conveyed nightmare stories of the unrest in the North. He observed with sadness and regret that policemen all over Ulster were being bombed and shot, almost on a daily basis. He pitied the wives and children left behind, but it did show him something with amazing clarity: the job of policing ever-increasingly dangerous streets, even in Dublin's fair city, was becoming a worldwide issue, and one in which police officers, their wives and dependants needed – deserved – some form of financial protection. So one bright may morning he dandered into Pearse Street Garda Station and asked to speak to the Duty Inspector.

Robert Harrison explained to the giant officer with temples of grey that, with the duties of police officers becoming more and more hazardous it would benefit each and every officer to sit down and seriously consider better protection for themselves, but especially for the family who would be left behind if the worst happened.

Harrison's main impetus in his new venture was not done to cash in on the atrocities of the North – that sort of mercenary behaviour was not part of his make-up – but he genuinely wanted to get a better and more financially rewarding deal for the men and women who patrolled Dublin's streets and who were putting their lives at risk day in and day out.

To say that he was inundated with applications for new policies, updates, and alterations to existing polices would be a gross understatement. A deluge of paperwork now balanced precariously on his desk. His workload quadrupled. In advising the previously unadvised police officers of Dublin city with care and discretion, within two years he was a registered millionaire. He had, indeed tapped a rich vein, finding and building up good one-to-one working relationships with the officers, whom he had found ill informed, frightened, and grossly underinsured.

Then he moved to the stockbroker belt, buying a luxurious period home only a few doors down from a rising rock star called Bono. He fulfilled his boyhood dream and bought himself a Porsche 911 Carrera – with cash – so that he and Aisling could travel in style to the many trade receptions and dinner parties to which they were invited.

He worked, he played, he enjoyed life, he worked even more, driving himself to higher and greater achievements, his life on a constant roller coaster, and one morning at three o'clock he found himself fighting for his life in a Dublin Intensive Care Unit following a heart attack. By right he should have died on the spot there and then, but some Divine intervention ensured that he would live to see the sun rise next morning.

It took four months and boundless loving care from Aisling to nurse him back to some degree of normality. His most often asked question over those painful four months was *what happened?* Every single day he thanked God that he had been spared, but what for? Four long months on his back, resting, restless, recuperating, he pondered his uncertain future.

'No more twenty-hour days for you m' lad!' said Aisling.

'No more million pound investments…'

'No more six-course dinner receptions…'

'Okay,' he joked, 'we really must cut down on the caviar – and no more Indian curries and brandy at midnight!'

'That's a deal,' she said, laughing, only too glad that they had at least the opportunity to rethink their future together. A serious look hatched Harrison's brow.

'I just thought that something I actually enjoyed doing wouldn't be doing me any harm. Not once did I feel stressed, or harassed. Busy, yes – up to my eyeballs, but never dangerously… life threatening…'

'Stress is a funny thing. Not funny ha ha; funny peculiar. Everyone has their breaking point,' said Aisling wisely, 'the problem is that you never know where it is until you're at it, and then it's too late.'

'We'll have to make some serious adjustments…' he said, now tired and needing a doze.

'Yes,' she said quietly, 'and you'll do well at whatever we decide; y' know y' can't keep a good man down!'

Robert Harrison had been thinking about that very thing. Downsizing, they called it nowadays. Something radical needed to be done. One more attack and it was *goodnight nurse*. He glanced half-heartedly over his financial position. He was wealthy, he knew that, but as he lay there in that bed, weak and tired he really did not know how much he was worth. Crazy, he thought. He thought of the teachers at school who wrote him off as non-academic, could do better, needs to improve, tends to be lazy. And now he could buy the school.

With a deep breath and a leap into the unknown Robert and Aisling gave most of their amassed fortune away. They donated enough to the hospital to be able to build and fully equip a new wing specialising in heart defects. The hospital authorities named it the Harrison Wing after a formal reception at which Robert drank only fizzy water. They donated to Special Olympics to improve sporting and social opportunities for those with special needs worldwide. And with the remainder they purchased two acres of barren, rocky ground and a derelict, tin-roofed cottage in Donegal overlooking the Atlantic.

Oddly, neither Robert nor his wife suffered any form of culture shock, but it didn't surprise them; they were still in wet old Ireland, the roads were still pot-holed, the people were still the friendly, quiet people they had always known. But oh, the breeze from the mighty Atlantic! The sharp, clear air of Donegal, reflecting the sun's light off the wild ocean that bombarded its coast was exhilarating. Each morning after breakfast Robert Harrison dandered down his little rutted lane to a sandy inlet and sat on the recumbent rocks, listening to the gulls and the wind ruffling the gorse.

Old Rua Flynn – as yet Robert hadn't worked out just how to take this old man in a long ragged coat and beard nearly the same length – ambled along the strand, his yellow collie sniffing at the rocks and seaweed, occasionally spurting across the sand to scatter a flock of lapwings.

'Fine morning!' Robert Harrison called, not really sure of the reply he would get. Rua Flynn looked up; he had been in a dream.

'Fine. Fine,' he agreed. Then after a pause and coming closer he said, 'Those were the fine eggs.'

Rua Flynn was known as a man of few words. Some said he had been a philosopher, or a professor, or a scientist. Some said his mind had snapped from studying the Bible too deeply. Robert Harrison strained to make sense of Flynn's compliment and then suddenly remembered Aisling having given the old man half a dozen eggs from their new Rhode Island Reds the week previous.

'Oh yea, the eggs! Great! Sure call any time.'

'They stayed in the pan and didn't go all runny like the oul' rubbish y' get nowadays,' Flynn added, while plucking a tuft of grey hair from his ear. Harrison remembered stopping off at a small farm in Tyrone to invest in six 'reds', as the farmer's fat wife had called them, wiping her crimson hands on her apron. Best wee layers in the country.

Aisling, on such grand praise as that of the sage and philosopher Rua Flynn, put up a little sign at the end of the lane: Free Range Eggs. *They Stay in the Pan!* She painted the plywood sign cream and Robert, in artistic mode, painted a happy hen smiling on her nest. 'A work of art!' laughed Aisling, admiring her husband's handiwork with her hands on her hips and her head tilted to the side.

Word spread, and soon every jovial, quietly-spoken wife in the townland of Knocknamara was buying her healthy, fawn eggs from Harrison's, filling the kitchen with the singing lilt of the Donegal accent.

After six months one hen died – of a heart attack, Robert assumed, the one they had named Henrietta – and after a decent burial at the back of an outhouse he drove back to the farm in Tyrone and, instead of replacing one for one, he splashed out and bought seven more. Aisling laughed until her sides were sore when Robert arrived back in the yard with seven new hens flapping and clucking in the back seat of the car. The new stock settled in well, and their soft cooing about the whitewashed sheds was comforting and homely, and now profitable.

Harrison, now the talk of the poultry world – well, in Knocknamara at least – fed his hens on scraps from the table – human food – and a good quality mash from Paddy the Cope's in Dungloe.

When the shop in the town – O'Garrity's – began stocking Harrison's eggs the demand was unending, but supply was now lacking. Robert, much to his astonishment yet quiet pride, had been strolling into town each morning with his wicker basket drumlined with eggs, depositing them with Josie O'Garrity, and by the time he left town they were all sold. Josie told him he had an book full of orders *for that man Harrison's eggs*.

'Must be what we're feeding them,' Aisling mused at the dinner table one evening, two perfectly poached eggs apiece.

'What – the hens or the locals?' Robert joked.

'The hens, stupid. Is it because each little feathered friend feels loved and wanted, and so they lay their eggs with loving care?'

'Don't go all soppy on me,' said Robert. 'This is a multi-million pound industry we're running here!' he laughed, looking up at the oil lamp flickering on the wall, the underside of the tin roof ceiling and the blue puffs of smoky downdraught from the chimney. 'Maybe it's because we feed them the best food available. Or maybe it's your wee inviting sign at the end of the lane. Sure even tourists and daytrippers are beginning to stop.' After a pause and a final mouthful of tea he looked at the antique Arizona clock ticking rhythmically on the mantle. 'It's near six. Time for the Angelus.'

'You've become a real Donegal man no doubt,' said Aisling, 'but we're going to need to buy more birds soon to keep up with demand.'

One beautiful summer evening as the smell of musky gorse aired the heather bogland, Robert Harrison sat on a rock, his favourite rock for sitting on when he had something to think about. Aisling brought two mugs of tea and a packet of chocolate biscuits down the lane to the inlet. The grandchildren were on their summer holidays and staying up late chasing each other through the bramble patch which, come another month or two would hang heavy with blackberries. The sounds of their cries and laughter at being scrabbed with the briars carried to the strand.

'What's on your mind?' Aisling asked.

'That oul' shed,' he said, pointing casually to the roofless barn at the back of the house. The thatch roof had long since collapsed in, rotting the wooden floor. The ground floor had been used as a byre at one time and the ties and mangers for the cows still stood, musky and dank, amid the last coat of lime that some long dead farmer had applied. 'I was thinking that if we put a bit of work into it we could renovate it and use it as a hen shed for about three or four hundred birds. Happy, well fed, good laying birds. We could call the business Harrison's Happy Hens, get a van, and start some serious distribution. What do y' think?' He was excited, almost twitching with ambition. Aisling rolled her eyes.

'Looks like here we go again!' she laughed, and hugged him under a yellow and orange sky.

AMBITION

I'VE OFTEN HEARD IT SAID that a son's life is spent trying to prove himself to his father. No matter how close or estranged a son and father become in life, it would seem that somewhere at the back of the son's head there lies a desire, a need – sometimes, I fear, an obsession – to win the approval of this most towering of figures. Even, it would seem, if the father is indifferent at best and downright disinterested at worst, the rule still applies.

Why this anomaly occurs, I don't know, but like all dealings with us humans there's no doubt some subtle and psychological reasoning, to be agonised about on Oprah, analysed in a BBC2 documentary, and skirmished over on Jerry Springer. Maybe it's to do with the amount of respect a father demands – or earns – in the boy's formative years; this gargantuan figure of awe and wonder, seemingly always doing the right thing and being able to do everything, someone to whom he literally looks up. Or is it fear? Fear of failure? Fear of a lashing, either with tongue or stick, even in this cotton-wool, wind-chime generation? Or are we simply genetically programmed to strive for the perfection that our most important elder seeks so that, as in man's ancient past, we stand a greater chance of survival in a hostile and dangerous environment? Survival. Now that may be the answer.

Personally, I don't know if these observations are true in one hundred per cent of cases, but one thing I do know: as far as Jamie Sutherland was concerned, it was true to the last detail.

Jamie was one of those artistic types, you know the kind; he would sketch the geography teacher and pass the caricature around the class and we all tried not to laugh out loud. Then eventually the teacher would find it, smile and make a fuss about finding out who had drawn him with such a big nose, confiscate it and take it home for a laugh with his wife that evening at the dinner table. Jamie had a precocious talent for observation and wit, and to all intents and purposes he was accepted as a happy, carefree child – just like the rest of us, I suppose. But that talent! It was a gift from God. I met him one day in Hillsborough forest, beside the lake with a sketch book and paints. I was out for a Sunday afternoon walk with my mum and dad and the dog. He had drawn the beautiful parish church in such miniscule, exact detail and was beginning to paint it in. It was magnificent. To be able to see the world with such clarity, and then transfer that beauty to resemble a three-dimensional object on a flat surface is indeed God-given. It was breathtaking, especially for someone like me who couldn't draw the curtains. My dad gave Jamie words of encouragement and told him to stick at it. He told Jamie he would be the next Picasso. Jamie just smiled his self-effacing smile and carried on painting, absorbed.

I remember even being absurdly jealous of how he could get on with the hard nuts in the school as well as the softies like me. One minute he was creating these beautiful delicate works of art and the next he was out getting tackled hard on the football pitch, and giving as good as he was getting. He seemed to be all things to all people. He was intelligent, emotional, good-looking and as deep as a well. And of course the girls swooned, waiting for their very own brush with genius. That's roughly how I remember him in school, and I really do believe he would have politely declined a date with the best looking girl in his class for his sketch book, his own company, the clouds and his paints.

Later, he told me he wanted to be a car designer. This meant he was destined to go to art college in Belfast and do the Bohemian student thing, growing his hair long and buying his clothes from Oxfam. But I knew he was up for it and it would be a dawdle for him to achieve his dream. I think his main ambition was, secretly, to have designed the car that his father would drive. I didn't understand then why that would be such a compelling factor, but it was. I didn't realise his overwhelming need to have his father take pride in him.

His father, a burly creation with a seventeen-inch collar and a chest like a bullock, on hearing that *his* son Jamie had applied for and was accepted into a five-year course at art college, threatened that if he ever caught Jamie drawing pictures of naked girls he would turf him out of the house on his ear. Those places are full of nothing but sex maniacs, communists and drug addicts, he said. I hope you're not turning into one of them *fruits*! His father's untimely criticisms gave Jamie second thoughts and sowed seeds of uncertainty, but he was an artist, he was the most creative person I've ever known and so the water, I thought, would eventually find its own level.

But it was as Jamie was sketching his final preparations for his first year at college, a sort of CV to show his future teachers, looking forward with some delight and trepidation to finding out all about Belfast, the Big Smoke and city life, when his father burst into his bedroom in anger with eyes like a vicious bull and shouted, 'Bloody well at it again are y'?'

'What?' asked Jamie, feeling his voice tremble in his throat.

'Useless!' his father said, lifting a carbon drawing of a musician playing a mandolin. He tossed it across the room. 'What's the point?' he went on. 'People who can draw are ten a penny. Why don't you go out and do something useful – like join the police?' As he stormed out, in his wake his father left clouds of doubt, grey and black, an end to everything Jamie had ever aspired to. And because his father had spoken, all plans were changed.

Jamie's heart sank to his feet. Eighteen years of fear, respect, confusion – call it what you like – now welled up in him like an acid stomach. If he pursued his artistic career an unbearable chasm of indifference and ill feeling would grow up between him and his father, and Jamie didn't know if he could cope with that alienation.

When Jamie told Sandra Walker, a red-haired girl whom he respected and got on well with in school, that he had changed his mind and would be applying to join the RUC she, after firstly thinking he was winding her up but later seeing the grim determination in his eyes, astutely suggested that he would be artistically frustrated for the rest of his life. 'If you have it in you,' she said, almost pleadingly, 'you have to let it out. And you'll not be able to do that when you're writing up your traffic accident reports and catching criminals.'

She said she couldn't imagine anything worse in life than to live your one opportunity in a state of frustration, denying yourself those things you really want to do and be, and as a by-product causing yourself so much inner conflict that you probably end up in bad health. Your life would, she argued, be lived in a general state of unhappiness. She joked and said that Jamie's life would become one long nervous breakdown.

'I'm afraid that if I don't get into car design on a professional level I'll end up teaching art to a bunch of uninterested scrotes,' he lied to her.

'Teaching scrotes – as you call them – would be even more fulfilling than strutting about like John Wayne and getting shot at.' At this stage Jamie wondered if she had fancied him all along and had been looking forward to art college together more as a romantic venture. But those thoughts now went to the bottom of the pile.

'The money's good…'

'Yes, if you work every hour the good Lord sends you…'

'Great pension…'

'If you live to see it…'

'It would be nice to see terrorism ended…'

'And do you think you're going to do that all by yourself? When have you become so interested in politics?'

'I *do* care,' he said, but his arguments were whitewash, and he knew it.

On dark nights, with the smell of Land Rover oil in his nose and his eyes streaming to stay open and awake, patrolling devious streets with cold steel machine gun, he would think of Sandra Walker's admonishments in the safety of the private study room at school. He didn't sketch anymore; his heart had gone out of it, nor did he elaborate on artistic theories to the hard boiled heads of his colleagues. Nobody was interested in the real colour of water on a lake, a blue shadow crossing a hillside, or the purple underbelly of a thunder cloud. They would know more about fish suppers and getting the load on and groping the station policewoman.

His father would ring the station occasionally to see how he was doing, especially if yet another policeman had been murdered or injured, or a security base had been mortared.

'I'm okay,' Jamie would say, his stomach heaving with silent sobs at the thought of a lost comrade, but not wanting to break down totally over the phone to his dad.

'Bad oul' times, eh?' his dad would say.

'Yea.'

Some of the bosses took a dislike to Jamie and seemed to make it their life's ambition to frustrate and demoralise him at every opportunity. One Inspector in particular – who wore a pink polo shirt and khaki shorts from March onwards, played golf and posed behind the façade of Born-Again Christianity while pinching fruit from the soldiers' canteen, and whose mousy hair was so perfectly styled it looked like it had been cut from cardboard – embarrassed and belittled Jamie, sometimes in the police canteen, but worse, sometimes in front of members of the public and colleagues. And it was because, when it boiled down to it, he knew that Jamie, a lowly Constable, could buy and sell him and come back for the change. Jamie hadn't yet learnt that idiot bosses see creative and effective employees as a threat, and their only way of keeping the threat low is to keep the employee demoralised and without motivation. And it was worthless to try and go one rank higher to the Chief Inspector and complain about the Inspector; he would find out soon enough that idiot bosses promote other idiots. Even so, Jamie hated the tension and tried to get each working day in with as little confrontation as possible, but the demeaning scowls continued in the corridors.

When Jamie married he soon had a daughter on whom he doted. She was a great distraction from everything else that bothered and annoyed him about his life and chosen career. The little girl – Lucy – was about three when her father was transferred from Belfast to a fortress in South Armagh; the result of too many demeaning scowls in too many corridors. An aggrieved boss's last resort was the dirty transfer, and so Constables and Sergeants who didn't conform found themselves walking the beat with eight soldiers on some Border road with an army helicopter hovering overhead for cover. It was a long way from helping old dears across the road.

Each morning at 8.30 on the dot Jamie stood at his locker in the glorified garden shed they called a locker room, getting his uniform on and preparing himself mentally for the day ahead. One morning as

Jamie was leaving home at 7.30 to be in work for 8.30 little Lucy began to cry. First a sob and then full blown, hysterical yelling.

'What's wrong, Sweetheart?' he said, playing with her and lifting her up to the ceiling while keeping an eye on the clock.

'Don't want you go work today,' she cried as he held her above him, jiggling her and making fun. Jamie could only laugh out loud. It was lovely to be loved.

'I'll be home at tea time,' Jamie reasoned, but Lucy cried on. He was going to be late for work, and he knew a patrol was due to leave for the Border at 8.45. It took a good ten minutes to settle her, which he eventually did, only on the promise of them all going to McDonalds for Happy Meals for tea. Ten minutes late. If he pushed it he could be in work for 8.40. The patrol might wait. As he raced southward and came to within a few miles of his destination a pall of sinister, black smoke rose on the horizon. It was his station. It was his locker room. A mortar, fired from a car park adjoining the station at 8.30 made a direct hit on the locker room and decimated everything. Jamie paled and sickened. His stomach turned sour. He thanked God in heaven above for his beautiful daughter, and tossed his breakfast up at the side of the road.

At some time Jamie, realising that he had spent over twenty years seemingly on the verge of mental and physical exhaustion, decided it was time, albeit late in the day, to think about another job. Teaching didn't seem too bad an option now, compared to the sixteen-hour working days, alienation and frustration he was enduring. These things, coupled with his emerging realisation that, even though he now genuinely wanted to help old ladies across the road, comfort victims of crime, reduce intimidation and cruelty, he saw that the RUC would, in years to come be consigned to history as the baddies of the Northern Ireland conflict. Even though he could put his hand on his heart and state that most of his friends and colleagues had the basic good of society at heart, and he was convinced that some of the best people in the country were in the RUC, but because the world now swayed towards giving land back to those from whom it had been taken, and forgave the actions of its freedom fighters, he knew that the RUC, having lost over three hundred officers would still be viewed as the bullies, the political puppets. He didn't want to be a baddy nor a bully; he just wanted to do his job, onerous and unsuited as it was.

He would look at some big, fat, brainless Constable who complained of being knackered after a week of night duty. And yet, Jamie thought, he didn't *look* tired, and after a night's sleep the big gorilla would probably be back to his usual bright-eyed, chips and gravy self. But Jamie's tiredness was absolute. He never slept properly because his brain was fixed in fifth gear, purple smudges would be a regular feature under his eyes, and sometimes he hadn't the energy to stand up. He looked continuously pale and lethargic, as if the very act of staying alive exhausted him.

And the concerned calls from his father continued to grow in momentum and frequency over the years.

'How's things?'

'Ach, workin' away.'

'I heard on the news —'

'Yea, a guy from B section —'

'You weren't involved?'

'No… I was on day shift. He died last night… His funeral's on Friday.'

'Terrible, terrible. Well, look after yourself, won't y'?'

'Yea, will do…'

'Are y' doin' any painting or drawing this weather?'

'Nah, but I might start again… start footerin' about, y' know?'

'Good.' his father said. And after a deep breath and a pause he asked, 'Would y' ever think of leavin' that oul' job… it's not getting' any better.' There was an even longer pause. A pause long enough that even Jamie's father coughed just to make sure the phone was still working. Jamie's chest heaved as if his throat was holding down an almighty wail. It was a pause just long enough for Jamie to remember Constable Murphy's brain exploding from a single shot from a sniper half a mile away, and holding the dying Constable in his arms. He remembered searching hopelessly for survivors in the rubble of the Shankill bombings, the little boy who had fallen off the back of a coal lorry which had in turn reversed unknowingly over the boy's chest, popping his eyes, the young man with his life in front of him with his throat slashed and his body dumped at the back of a community centre on the New Lodge Road. The pause was long enough to remember the blank, uncomprehending look on a boss's face when Jamie had expressed some new, creative idea that the boss couldn't understand. He remembered the senior officer who had a *quiet word* with him and asked him in all seriousness if he shouldn't seek psychiatric help. And his belief that most of the stress within the RUC wasn't caused by the IRA, but by untrained senior officers to whom the concept of man-management would come as a shock. The un-understanding, flat, untired eyes of colleagues, the drivel and the gossip. The drivel and the gossip. The drivel and the gossip. And the tiredness. Oh, the tiredness…

'Do you remember, Dad,' Jamie said timidly, and it was as if some other life form had invaded his mouth and was speaking for him. 'When I was going to go to art college and you didn't like the idea and you said that I should go and do something useful… like join the police…?'

There was another silence. Life seemed to have become a collection of silences. Jamie's chest fluttered like the beginnings of a heart attack. Could he now actually be preparing to get twenty years' frustration and silence off his chest in one fell swoop, no matter what the consequences? It needed to be said, but was he about to reverse the run of his life to date and reprimand his own father?

'Do you, Dad?'

Silence.

'No…' his father said, 'I can't say I remember that.'

APPARITION

I STUDIED MY PIMPLY TEENAGE FACE in the bathroom mirror. What a
mess! Only yesterday my father had snarled at me and told me to go
out and get a breath of fresh air or I'll be in an early grave. He hated
to see me stuck up in my bedroom with my T.Rex and tape recorder
and teenage testosterone. I had to admit my face was ghostly pale, but
then I was sixteen, a pop star of the future and allergic to fresh air. My
life up until then seemed to have been spent strumming mindless
chords, trying to make my voice waver like Bolan, and saving up every
penny I could get my hands on for my own Strat. The evening before,
at a gathering of like-minded and similarly-faced friends (one of whom
– without the acne – being a girl who was probably single-handedly
responsible for the turbulent hormones now coursing my bloodstream
and causing the aforementioned facial eruptions) I had sipped a glass
or two of Martini. It was the in drink then for anyone who didn't like
beer, or who thought lager and Guinness uncouth. Spirits were a bit
too heavy and an admission of adulthood. The only reason I'd tried
Martini was because, well, I liked the lettering on the label of the green
bottle, and of course, also, when the girl of my passion was drinking it
and offering it freely at the party, how could I resist? (Anytime,
anyplace, anywhere, as they say…)

Before me in the mirror (actually it was only an unframed plate of
mirror glued to the gloss paint above the small bathroom sink) my face
suddenly changed from spotty and ashen to spotty and crimson. God!

That was so embarrassing! I cringed, feeling the shiver of mortification slip like an eel up my back as I grudgingly remembered my grand entrance to the party at Lynn's house the evening before. You see, what I wanted to wear more than anything and impress my friends with was one of the new trendy pullovers that were taking the fashion world by storm. Boy, I wanted a turtleneck! All the coolest dudes in the rock and pop world were wearing them on Top of the Pops and in Jackie magazine and yet their availability didn't seem to stretch further than Carnaby Street. Absolutely no-one I knew had one, but I knew it would only be a matter of time before they would be as common as custard. I wanted to be the first in the town to sport that suave neckline which wasn't quite a polo neck and yet wasn't as staid and traditional as a school uniform V-neck. It was halfway between the sublime and the meticulous and it looked lush. I imagined the attention I would attract. Them all sitting there with their cans of Tennents and Harp and Paisley-pattern shirts with round collars and chunky ties and me with my turtle neck and sports coat, sipping Martinis and standing informally beside Lynn chatting philosophically about Neitzsche and Da Vinci.

But I was forgetting one thing. I was forgetting that I was living in Backwoodstown, Smallville, Northern Ireland where the most trendy fashion statement was still a three-piece tweed suit and a walking stick and hair parted in a fire-breaker middle shade. By the time turtlenecks would arrive here they would have gone out of fashion everywhere else in the world.

But what if, I had mused the previous evening as I pulled on my flares and zip-up boots, what if I simply put my green school pullover on backwards? My God – it would become a turtleneck! My grey sports coat – the one with hideously sharp-angled lapels which tapered into a point at each shoulder – would hide the V-neck gap at the back! What a peach idea. Lush. It was time for some improvisation. So I walks into the party – late, so as to make The Big Entrance – with all eyes on my new turtleneck, acting nonchalant but already sweating under Lynn's dad's newly installed oil-fired central heating – and before I knew it Lynn, as the perfect hostess, had taken my jacket and handed me a Martini. Roars of laughter erupted from everyone in the room before I had time to realise exactly what they all found so hilarious. I instantly cursed that new heating system; what was wrong with burning coal in a nice open fire, or the dry, suffocating heat from electric storage heaters that somehow only warmed small areas of the room – and your body – at a time?

'Were y' on the drink before y' came out James, old son?' shouted Alexander Harrington. He was a ghoul, a pseudo-intellectual who had grown a beard at fifteen and spoke at everyone in his condescending Ulster/English accent. Nothing worse. Everyone was now pointing and sniggering, pointing and sniggering with Tennents to their lips and red wine in their hands giggling and Pink Floyd's One of these Days reaching a climax and me standing like a bin lid in the middle of the room with my school pullover on backwards.

Now, as Halloween approached and dark at four o'clock, the harsh bathroom light with no lampshade – just a cold white bulb – rendered my blushing face and gaunt eyes menacingly similar to The Scream. Any minute now my two mates from down the street – Joe Smart and Thomas King – would be tapping at the door and we'd spend the dark evening swathed in the yellow glow of the one light from Mrs Baxter's sweet shop on the main street, kicking stones against the wall and whispering and fantasising about the girls in the town we'd love to lumber, and lying about our conquests and ruining good, chaste girls' reputations forever.

'Who shaves y'?' laughed Joe Smart as I answered the door, letting the biting night air invade the house.

'Myself; it's cheaper,' was the accepted reply.

'Comin' out?' asked Tommy King, but it was a mere formality and only a well rehearsed question which wasn't a question. Obviously I was coming out; there was nothing worth watching on either of the two TV channels, I'd done my Geography homework and was fed up being jealous of the sunny, orange-growing counties of California, and anyway, my older brother was engrossed in tense study about something and my morose father was still unable to cope following the sudden death of his wife – our mother – only two years before. I grabbed my bomber jacket from the row of six-inch nails which passed for pegs under the stairs and shouted up to my younger brother, 'Sam… are y' comin' out?' By the sudden leaping like a young gazelle down the stairs three at a time I knew that he, too, was relieved to be escaping the oppressive gloominess of the house.

'Waddlewedo forra laugh?' said Joe, picking his nose.

'I wish there was some girls about.' said Tommy despondently. 'I fancy a grope.' He was probably the most sexually-advanced one of the four of us and we respected his alleged experience. But it was true; our own little Nowheretown wasn't renowned for its proliferation of stunning and promiscuous females. So when sex – or at least ill-informed adolescent inter-gender contact – is unavailable, the male psyche turns to the next item on the agenda: 'I see Missus Baxter has a big tray of toffee apples made. They're covered in coconut! Who fancies one?' asked Joe, now quite excited. I was on my way back into the house to see if Dad would lend me a shilling when I had a fantastic idea, but I didn't jump to enlighten the boys, remembering with another quick flush that my last fantastic idea (remember the V-neck?) wasn't such a fantastic idea after all. But being the patron saint of Amusing Ways to Pass the Time I eventually betrayed my initial hesitance and suggested, 'What about making a ghost and scaring the crap outta people?'

'Aye, let's do it!' laughed Joe, forgetting about the coconut-covered toffee apples lined up proudly like soldiers on Mrs Baxter's baking tray. Thomas, always the doubter, stuck his hands deep in his pockets and kicked the edge of the doorstep. 'What will we make it outta? Where will w' put it?' he asked, but I knew from years of practice that if I ignored Thomas's initial indifference and pressed on, he would eventually come round to my way of thinking.

'We need two poles; one about ten feet long and the other about two or three feet,' I said with exaggerated interest for Tommy's sake. 'We'll tie them into a cross and then drape a big white sheet over it. Then we'll hide behind the forest wall and when a car comes along we'll run along and hold the thing up and scare the sh—'

'Great idea!' laughed Joe, giggling at the thought of it. Thomas smiled with subdued interest but I knew I had won him over and he was dying to get started. Sam, my wee brother, nodded in quiet agreement and said nothing.

'My da's got stacks a wood; I'll go and raid the shed and get the poles and nails,' said Joe, getting keener by the moment to witness the terrified looks on the faces of unsuspecting motorists. Tommy and Sam stood chatting in the cold of the front porch about Status Quo's new single while I nipped upstairs and whipped the white sheet off my bed, sneaking it out the back door.

When we had constructed the tall cross with the poles (the long one turned out to be Joe's dad's flag pole and was loaned on the solemn promise that it would be returned in tact to the shed before the Twelfth), we draped my sheet over the framework, and as Sam held it up we all retreated for a better inspection. But it had no head; the sheet just hung there like a Boy Scout's tent on a wet weekend; formless, headless. Sam skipped upstairs and got one of his old pullovers – it was a great idea – and we wrapped it tightly round the top of the pole as a sort of demented skull. When we hoisted our ghoulish invention up again it looked amazing – haunting almost; almost as frighteningly haunting as a teenage son first thing in the morning. We cackled in the dark at our ingenuity and soon we were transporting our very own Frankenstein monster out of town to a dark, secluded stretch of road, bordered on one side by the high demesne wall of the forest park, chucking it into the hedge at the other side of the road every time a car came along.

We selected the spot for the ambush, overgrown with tall leafless birches and oaks. An owl sailed through the air towards the trees from its hunting fields, silent and mysterious.

Joe and Tom threw the ghost over the wall and we all climbed over the green gate, dropping into the hushed forest. We gathered, like escaped prisoners, and decided upon our plan of action.

'Who'll carry it first?' somebody asked. Eager for first blood and the privilege of leadership I volunteered. We could hardly contain ourselves with anticipation as we waited at the edge of the musky forest for our first victim. Dripping dank nature enfolded around us, beautiful but terrifying, our faces wan in the moonlight.

'Wish a had a fag,' said Tom. Sam said that the drivers would see the smoke and give us away, and we all laughed again.

'Here's somebody!' Tom whispered, and we all instantly froze, cocking our ears, and craning our necks like parrots. He was right.

'Right! Up she goes!' I said. And Sam, for no apparent reason, added, 'Up she goes, the colour's blue, every time she bumps she bounces...' We didn't know what he was talking about, but in the adrenalin-fuelled nervousness of the situation we all laughed anyway.

The apparition, like a Twelfth of July banner, the sails of a mighty galleon, Jesus on the cross, the American flag at Iwo Jima, rose slowly and defiantly into the night sky. We stood, ours hearts thumping in our temples, listening to the car's spluttering engine, and then the lights struck. Oh! The lights! It was wondrous! They shone gloriously on our creation, luminous and ghostly and all at once we were running like blue blazes, me holding the thing on high and it flapping and levitating in the car's headlights. It was magical to wonder, to visualise, what the driver of the car was seeing. As we crunched over dead branches, slithered on decomposing clumps of brown fern and pine needles, laughing and breathless we stopped only when the car had passed, leaving the scene once again in darkness.

We couldn't speak for a good two minutes, wanting to laugh but trying to do it quietly. Joe leaned helplessly against the wall, wiping tears of mirth from his eyes. I feared he was going to have an asthma attack, while my brother Sam was up and eager to do it again. Joe, through spluttered titters, volunteered to carry it next time. Tommy King, never easily impressed, admitted defeat and held his sides complaining that all the laughing had given him a stitch. I was glad that this most recent idea of mine had already proven a towering success.

We hauled the ghost back to the start. We waited patiently for the next car. In the meantime I made a suggestion.

'What if me and Tommy hide in the hedge at the other side of the road – then we can see the fright on their faces? Joe and Sam could work the ghost okay, couldn't you?'

'Okay,' said Joe. 'As long as we get a chance to watch next time.'

Tommy and I ducked down behind the tall, unkempt hawthorn hedge. Behind us were Hughie McIntosh's ploughed fields. I looked over my shoulder at the polished furrows glistening in the frosty air of an October night, and shivered. I couldn't wait to get telling the story of our nocturnal exploits in school the next day.

And soon, after about ten minutes, a weary engine could be heard, weaving through the far-off drumlins. Some innocent driver didn't know it yet, but was soon going to get the fright of his life – we hoped so, anyway.

'Here's one comin'!' I shouted to Joe and Sam behind the wall and slowly the creature rose, and rose, to reach its full height; erect and fearless. The car got closer. The lights glowed brighter. I could hear Tommy's stifled chuckles beside me as we watched the car approach and as the headlights lit up the bed sheet the ghost took off, floating behind the wall, now at full speed, as the old woman at the wheel glared in terror, craning her neck round at an impossible angle and accelerating away at full speed towards the town.

'What did it look like?' shouted Joe from the darkness of the forest but neither Tommy nor I could utter a word because of the stitches of laughter biting into our bellies. Eventually we were able to tell them it looked lush, and now both Joe and Sam begged to get to watch.

'One more time,' I, as leader of the pack, said. 'Then we'll swap round – okay?' So Tommy and I concealed ourselves behind the hedge again, listening to the rustling of the ghost being returned to the start.

The road wasn't busy and it seemed an age before the next car came. To cheer us up Joe shouted, 'What happens if somebody has a heart-attack?' We hadn't taken this grim possibility into our reckoning, but we had gone too far, we were in too deep and having too much fun to backtrack now, so after the initial millisecond of doubt and uncertainty we didn't give our possible coronary victim another thought. Just then an engine sounded in the distance, travelling quite quickly. I could have told them it was a Ford.

'Here's another one!' I shouted to Joe and Sam, cupping my hands. The car approached. Yes, I thought smugly, it definitely is a Ford. The headlights loomed brighter, the ghost was hoisted. Our hearts were beating the heads off us. The ghost looked beautiful, and I took a second or two just to admire it and relish the moment.

The car accelerated, and accelerated, closer and closer, the blazing yellow lights now fully trained on my bedclothes. The ghost was about to take flight when the car skidded to a halt, burning rubber right along the middle of the road and the black shapes of two figures shot from the car at lightning speed.

'Cops!' I shouted. '...run!'

Tommy and I turned and began hoofing it up the ploughed field. I looked back over my shoulder and with the corner of my eye I saw the ghost fall as if it had been shot, sprawling over a tall rhododendron bush, while imagining Joe and Sam legging it into the undergrowth. Tommy and I were both fit youngsters then, and we wasted no time covering ground, even though I cursed modern fashion for inflicting high-heeled zip-up boots upon us feckless teenagers, which made sprinting over the ruts and rises of a ploughed field painfully impossible.

In the blind panic of trying to reach the safety of the ridge at the top of the field, knowing that two angry cops were on our tails, I heard a sharp metallic crack and one of them shouted, 'Stop or I'll shoot!' In our adrenalin-fuelled bid for freedom we kept running, but Tommy eventually, through panting gasps, managed to say, 'Jim... we'd better stop.' I halted and stood there, and as our captors trundled up to us I, for some reason put my hands high above my head.

Gestapo-like flashlights glared in our eyes, reflecting sometimes on shiny peaks and polished tunic buttons, as a barrage of inane questions were spat at us.

'What's yer name?'

'Jim Burrows.'

'What age are y'?'

'Sixteen.'

'What are yez playin' at?'

'We were just...' and even as I spoke I was aware of my own observation that if you put the word just in an explanation it makes what you are saying sound like a lie, so I kept quiet and let Tommy answer.

To this day I am convinced that the scene in which we found

ourselves part of in that lonely ploughed field on that autumn night would make a fantastic painting. I wish some artist would depict it. Like a Goya, the dramatic silhouette of four figures on the horizon, two of them smaller, with their hands pointed skyward and the other two officious and brutal, aiming their sub-machine guns at the trembling youths.

All the while the other squat little Reserve Constable was interrogating Tommy and making one hell of a big issue out of it, with threats and curses and the torchlight flashing. They tossed us into their nice shiny Ford Escort, proud of their night's catch, and escorted us off to parade in front of our parents. While they spoke to each other in their concealed police lingo, Tommy and I sat dumbly, wondering if they really would have shot us in the back. It was sad, and disillusioning to think that as we drove back to face the music with our parents, (well, as far as I was concerned, only my dad) only ten miles away the most ruthless terrorist organisation in the world was planning and executing atrocities that would stun the western world and here were Laurel and Hardy as the Keystone Cops threatening to shoot two unarmed teenage pranksters in the back.

We pulled up outside Tommy's house and he was led disconsolately to the front door. I knew I would hear the full story of what was said the next morning at the bus stop. The fat officer who stayed in the car with me kept grilling me as to what we had been playing at and telling me I should've had more sense and what would have happened if some driver would have had a weak heart and suffered a heart attack and died but I couldn't speak for my trembling, apologetic chin.

I feared the wrath of my father. He would probably murder me slowly and agonisingly. He'd had enough trouble in his life over the past two years and now here I was heaping on more. I was sad also that, thinking about my mother, I had let her down and brought our grieving family to the notice of two officious RUC men, who will probably be boasting of their triumphs to everyone they meet for the next fortnight. 'Wait'll y' hear this… we caught young Burrows the other night…' they'll say. '…and his mother not cold in her grave…' We'll be the talk of the town, I knew, as I sat with my hands between my knees in the shoe polish and gun oil smell of the back seat of that police car, feeling, not for the first time, that life had run away from me.

Dad took an interminable time to answer the door. I could imagine him prising himself up from the sofa, stuffing the Radio Times back under the cushion and putting his shoes on. The cop held my arm in case I'd do a runner. When the door opened I said *I'm sorry Dad* before the cop could speak. Boy was I in for it.

'Is this your son, Mister… Burrows?'

'Yes. Why? What's wrong?' My dad's eyes widened; confused, terrorised.

'We found him out the road with a corpse…' (Corpse? I felt like saying. It wasn't a corpse. But then exaggeration seemed to be part of this promotion-seeker's make-up.) As he spoke, from behind his back, like a magician, he produced the head of the ghost – Sam's old pullover – and held it out to Dad as a trophy of his efficiency. I could see my dad's eyes widen even further and his chin drop and his lip tremble and in his bereaved state of mind he put two and two together and worked out that the pullover was indeed his son's and that the corpse to which this efficient officer was referring was also his dead son, Sam.

'Where's Sam?' Dad blurted, the blood draining from his face. 'Jim – where's Sam?' I quickly assured Dad that Sam was okay, now remembering for the first time that Sam and Joe were probably still hiding in the forest and having a good laugh at the thought of Tommy and I as prisoners of war.

'This fella was trying to scare motorists…' the officer went on, probably sensing that his promotion wasn't far off, but my dad wasn't interested in the man's self-importance anymore. He was only too relieved that Sam was alive and well and he knew that the prank was just so typical of my zany sense of humour, that he almost burst out laughing in the officer's chubby face.

RUNNING

WHEN I WAS A BOY I USED TO RUN. I ran everywhere. I ran to the playing fields at the other side of the village to play football with my friends. I ran wildly and madly over sand dunes on a Sunday trip to Tyrella beach, or even when my mother or father would give me an errand to the shops I would dash out the door like something not wise and run the whole way there and back. At every burst of primal acceleration, dodging pedestrians and skipping three flagstones at a time I would hear my mother or father's wasted warnings follow in my slipstream: 'Watch y' don't fall!' or 'Take yer time willya!'

I was Geordie Best, Stirling Moss, Tarzan, and Illya Kuryakin all rolled into one as I dashed and darted through streets and fields. I had no time for walking. Both my knees were forever crisscrossed with scars long and short, deep and superficial from tumbles on the tarmac. One scar of which I was particularly proud came about as I ran from the house one Twelfth of July morning on hearing the first of the bands heading for the assembly point. I tripped on the step and crash-landed on my right knee. The rest of the celebratory day was spent with a tear of self pity in my eye, a crude bandage the length of my leg, and my father admonishing me and telling me that he told me that would happen if I didn't take my time.

The front door of our house seemed to act as a springboard for my running. The second I was free from it I jettisoned myself into my own world of raw speed; free, like a young antelope, my legs light as air, my feet springing with each luscious stride, my fringe flopping in my eyes, splashes of sweat on my forehead and upper lip. I loved it.

'That wee fella never takes his time,' I could hear the old men and women tut behind me as I whizzed past. I heard one declare, 'He's as fast as one of them Harlem Gobstoppers!' Some of the older boys hanging around the street corner would shout as I passed, 'Hey boy, y' dropped somethin'.' And when I looked round they would shout, 'Too late – the flies are on it!' But I didn't care. I ran on.

I ran to catch the bus to school in the mornings and when it stopped near the school I ran the remaining few hundred yards, overtaking weary pupils walking with their heads disconsolately down, despising every step up the school's driveway. But I ran on. And when school finished for the day – after countless warnings from teachers not to run in the corridors – I ran back to the bus stop, eventually only freed when the bus stopped in my village and I sprung free and bolted home, my schoolbag bouncing merrily on my back.

I suppose it was just me. Everything had to be done in a hurry. I was impatient, unsettled, keen to get on with life and see what was round the next corner, and so running was probably the physical outlet for my inner restlessness. My father used to tell me that even as a baby in my cot or pram my legs never stopped kicking and jerking. He says I kept going forty to the dozen. He was sure I was going to be a professional footballer, or at least some kind of athlete.

I did love playing football. It was a chance to run for ninety minutes without others telling you to slow down and take your time. It was sheer, virgin pleasure to gallop across a flat pitch with its short grass and twenty-one like-minded athletes. To me, the skills and tactics required for the beautiful game were secondary to the joy of simply running. To outpace an opponent. To get to the ball before someone else by using my two legs and animal speed was one of my greatest joys.

I won a running race once. Just once. It was at a Sunday school sports day in the leafy grounds of Hillsborough fort. The eleven-year-olds had to run the entire distance round the lake – about a mile – along the bumpy, rustic path. It was a sunny Saturday and as we lined up Michael Thompson was the favourite, although bets were strictly forbidden. Even the Sunday school teacher, Mister Wilkinson, said casually to Michael, 'You should win this hands down, Michael m' lad.' I was slightly deflated on hearing this outburst of favouritism, but my anticipation for running a race soon elated me again.

When Mister Johnston, the minister, waved his QUB scarf in the air we were off. Down the slight incline to the boat house, along the flat straight at the back of the church where fishermen froze in mid cast as we passed, then turning right at the marshy dip full of skunk cabbages and then a straight section towards the Mossy. There was some pushing and nudging; some runners after a collision with another runner went sprachling into the rhododendrons and used the foul as an excuse to give up and walk back to the field. Half a mile round and some of the less fit children pulled out, using the age-old oaks as supports for their exhausted puffing.

At the head of the field there was Michael Thompson, looking nonchalant and confident, spitting occasionally. Then Ashley Thompson, Michael's twin brother, but not identical. Then me. And I was enjoying every stride. By the time we got to the bridge Ashley had taken a stitch and no matter how many calls of encouragement from Michael to keep running, it'll go away if you keep running, Ashley had to drop out, leaving only Michael and I to battle it out at the front. So we skipped effortlessly through the trees on the sun-splattered paths, feigning adult seriousness and determination.

But I didn't really want to win. That was my problem, you see, and it always had been. It was just in my nature, I suppose. That's why I never ran competitively; I just didn't like to see people defeated and hurt. Silly, isn't it? In those days I would have done anything not to hurt someone and that – stupidly – was why I didn't make a particular effort to win anything. My competitiveness was zero. For me the elation of winning something was overshadowed by watching someone's face in defeat. I was happier to see someone else collect the prize, someone else being cheered, someone else lift the trophy.

Stupid as it may seem, and I'm almost embarrassed to say, but I always felt sorry for peoples' feet. Yes, feet. Maybe it's because I see feet as the most unattractive part of the human body; bent out there at the end of your leg, with five curled up hideous toes, bony ankles and hardened skin. Feet just have nothing going for them. And when I'm walking alongside someone and look down at their feet, those lumps of fat and bone carrying us where we want to go, I find myself softening towards that person, pitying them almost, just because they happen to have feet. If I'm in the middle of a heated argument with someone and I happen to glance at their feet, well, I lose the will to argue and let them win. Except on this summer's day in Hillsborough forest. And it was only because Michael Thompson goaded me as we ran. He managed to whisper deviously through his laboured panting, 'You couldn't beat a sick elephant, Burrows, y' wee fruit!'

I didn't exactly know what he meant, but it sounded a good enough taunt to give me the impetus to burst forward with such a spurt of speed that for a second I left him in my wake. It was such a satisfying feeling, like when you pull on an old pair of jeans and find a tenner in the pocket. Then he slowly caught up with me again, but my blood was raging in my veins. I dare not look at his feet! I wanted to win. I had to win. Then sometime I would find out what it was he had called me. On the final straight I burst forward again with all guns blazing in front of a hundred Sunday schoolers and beat Michael Thompson by a good five yards.

'I didn't know you could run like that, young Burrows,' Mister Wilkinson confessed as he handed me the shiny medal.

'I just like running,' I said, smiling.

Throughout Secondary School years I kept running. For buses. To the shops. Just for fun. I used to say I was away for a walk, but really I ran. As I grew into young manhood I realised that to onlookers I looked a bit silly, this fully grown man running around the streets like somebody who should be locked up. I knew that an adult running sparks panic in an onlooker, who thinks that the man is running away from some danger, and so the onlooker's immediate reaction is to drop everything and start running too. So I bought the best running gear I could afford, and the new style spongy trainers gave an even lighter spring to my tread – just like running on air. The soles seemed to catapult my foot forward with each step. It was sublime.

The local police Sergeant must have thought it sublime as well. He stopped me one day, with his smart green uniform and three gold stripes gleaming on his arm and said, 'You're a fit youngin, so y' are. Y'd make a good officer.' I thought he meant an officer in the army so I said, 'I'd be no good in the army.'

'A police officer, son. RUC. Would y' ever think about it?'

Both my parents went ballistic when I told them I was thinking about joining the police. I tried in vain to emphasise the sporting aspects and opportunities of the job, arguing that you actually got time off to play and improve your sport. Imagine that – running and getting paid for it! Competing in competitions throughout the world. Where else would that happen, I ask you? What other job could offer such opportunities?

I came first in all the fitness tests at the training centre in Enniskillen. They called it The Depot then. There was no blind competitiveness there, but my natural fitness – built up since those days as a baby kicking the sides of my pram – stood by me and made it easy.

I believe that as the twelve-week training course came to a close the bosses, or authorities (to give them the title they prefer), organised that my first posting would be to some station in Belfast so that I would be close to the police's own sports and training facilities. I usually made it on to the Divisional football team as well, which meant even more time off from onerous police duties. And in my spare time I ran.

One night on patrol in west Belfast I was passenger and Jim Docherty was driving. We had been talking casually about the looming hunger strike, Jim's up-and-coming promotion to sergeant, and the new, easy-on-the-eyes policewoman who'd recently joined our section. Jim slowed the heavy Land Rover down for a speed ramp. Just as we were almost at a complete stop there was first a blindingly bright flash to my left, then a second later my so-called armour-plated door exploded with one almighty crash and bang. There was a sound of metal being mangled, more smaller electrical flashes and above it all I heard Jim's wail of shock.

Then I was deafened. Shrapnel from somewhere had struck Jim and he was slumped over the steering wheel, unconscious. At least I hoped he was unconscious. Other than being unable to hear anything I remained amazingly alert. In fact I would say that my senses had never felt so acute, before or since. I saw that something was burning under the dashboard, and I had the presence of mind to unhitch the fire extinguisher and put the flames out. I was aware that the back-up vehicle's crew were trying to rescue us, while they, in turn came under fire from a sniper hiding half a mile away. The fumes from burning acrid plastic made me choke and gag.

It was tar black in that cabin but within seconds I noticed a gooey, thick liquid had splashed all over me. At first I thought it was engine oil. I turned on the interior light – still working – to see what state Jim was in so that we could both help ourselves get out of there before the whole shebang went up in flames. In the uncertain pale light I saw that the liquid was my own blood and that my two legs were severed and mangled on the floor, leaving only two smouldering stumps, gristle, and scorched muscle. My heroic thoughts of saving Jim and myself slowly faded as I began to dream of sunny days in Hillsborough forest, I heard voices of people I knew in the past, the police Sergeant inviting me to join up…

❖

That was twenty years ago. I managed to learn to walk again, but most times I just use my trusty old wheelchair. Most places have become disabled-friendly now compared to what it was like when I first lost the legs. I even hear that in the future every door in every house will have to be made wide enough for wheelchair access. So things are looking up.

And some nights I dream. I dream that I am running. In my dreams I can run for miles without taking a breath or slowing down. There is a permanent smile on my face as I dart past pedestrians on the footpaths, or when I dream I'm playing football. My feet trot along country roads and lead me to mountain paths and forest footways. My hair bobs along with every footfall and under the trees spots of sunlight pepper the ground before me. I know that as I'm dreaming my stumps twitch and run with me, and when I wake up with my bed saturated in sweat I know I've been running. I *know* I've been running.

SOMETIMES

…sometimes he can be a right moody bugger y'know like he can go for weeks on end and be as pleasant and thoughtful asking me if I need anything done about the house and telling me I've classy makeup on my eyes which makes me look like a supermodel and that a particular lipstick makes my lips look luscious and sexy and I tell him that nobody else ever noticed those little things before and when I'm feeling down he tells me how he makes himself feel better when he's down like going to an ATM and reading the discarded receipts and finding out that everybody else is in the red as well or going into Easons and buying a Porsche mag and making sure everyone in the queue sees it or going to the bank and withdrawing a hundred pounds out of his savings and walking about with it in his pocket he says that makes him feel good but I say that all my problems aren't financial so he says I'm lucky and at those times I want to kiss him and cuddle him and delve headlong into his mind because it's as if he can read my mind and knows what to say at the right time to make me feel good so I hold him and feel him strong in my arms and whereas he sometimes looks shyly away under his eyes I just know that underneath the coy glances and self-demeaning looks there's this bottomless powerhouse of toughness and strength that makes the shyness seem more shy and the toughness seem tougher especially when he's in the company of others like my friends whom he doesn't really know and he doesn't really want to be with but he grins and bears it for me and I watch him making the effort to be friendly with people and he makes a good job of telling jokes and saying some of the wittiest things you'd ever hear but I know that deep down he would prefer it to be just me and him alone in the house with two glasses of Merlot and some nibbles and us lying on the couch watching a DVD or one of his vast collection of videos that he recorded over the years but which will be soon obsolete what with DVDs and soon to be HVDs that'll make even DVDs obsolete but whatever we lie and watch we seem to find a common thread that both of us love and we titter and laugh and if he doesn't understand something that's happening in the plot because sometimes he's not that quick to catch the joke or the subtlety in things and I have to explain it to him and then he says Oh yea I gettit now and we'll laugh and I'll ask do you fancy a cup of coffee but he declines because he says if he drinks coffee so late he'll be up peeing in the middle of the night and he has this weird theory that every time you are wakened during a night's sleep you loose an hour's benefit so if you're wakened eight times during the night then the next day it will feel as if you haven't been to bed at all so that's why I don't make coffee but he takes another sip of Merlot and looks at me under those deep eyes and I know that he probably has another theory going on in his head about him and me upstairs later but that's him always thinking things out and making theories like saying that a smile from a beautiful woman can brighten a dead man's soul and that a man is at his most vulnerable when his trousers are round his ankles and that all art is based not on beauty but honesty and he says that he's not holding his breath waiting to go to heaven because it couldn't possibly be better that the great times we have together so if heaven isn't a million times better he doesn't want to go which is lovely of him to say and makes me feel good and wanted and when we're together I feel complete and loved and sexy but when I'm not with him I feel lonely even in a crowded street and even food doesn't taste the same as when I'm with him and I swear I could eat caviar and venison in the company of Lords and Ladies till the cows come home but they would be tasteless compared to the Big Mac and chips and Coke at a crowded McDonald's on a wet Saturday afternoon just knowing that of all the people that have ever lived or that are living now the man across the table from me taking great gulps of Coke and getting dabs of Ronald's secret recipe on his chin is the one person I've loved most in my life and I know that I couldn't ever love anyone anymore than now and I'm always telling him that he's attractive even though he doesn't believe me and argues that he was last in the queue when the good looks were handed out but I tell him he's loving kind well-mannered honest caring loyal soft-hearted sexy and possessive and another one of his theories is that when two people love one another as much as we do there's no need for words because our souls speak to one another and that's why we can't lie or try to bluff the other because our insides know what the other is thinking and feeling and our souls are always telling the truth even if our lips aren't so he says that you shouldn't use the word love too lightly but if you genuinely feel it you should say it and say it and say it and I think he's right because the word love is like the word genius that has been watered down and watered down until it's now just a throwaway word that two chavs say on the Oprah and Trisha shows after they've kissed and made up for the sake of the cameras and national TV and it's flogged in every love song and every episode of every TV soap but I can see where he's coming from because he's a typical Scorpio who finds relationships difficult at first but when love does comes round it will be powerful and intense and forever but as I was saying at the start every now and again for no apparent reason he will lapse into such black moods and all he seems to want to do is hurt me I mean he has never once laid a vicious hand on me I must tell you but sometimes he can insult and insinuate so bitterly it's as good as a slap on the mouth or a fist in my stomach and he will keep going and keep going bringing up things I did in the past that meant nothing and things I said that I didn't mean any harm by but like I say he's a typical Scorpio who stores everything away in the back of his head until it's needed some day to prove a point or win an argument and he'll keep on until I start crying and pleading with him and telling him I love him no matter what but in these dark depressions he doesn't want to know and he says there's no use harping on about love this and love that because life's not as simple as that but when he sees me in the absolute depths of despair he seems to come out of his trance and then he apologises and says that he was well aware that he was hurting me but couldn't stop it's as if sometimes he needs to rid himself of ghosts and bad episodes in his life as if every now and again the past creeps up on him and angers him with all its injustices and he probably in turn takes the anger and pain out on me and I wish at those times there was some sort of help or therapy he could get or something I could magically do for him but when he gets back to loving me like nobody has ever loved me before he says he can't promise that it won't happen again but hopes that it won't ...

WHAT COMES ROUND

Dan O'Donnell from Derrydruel was skipping along the Meenacarn Road when he saw his best friend leaning over the cemetery wall, smoking the stub of a cigarette.

'Mornin' Dec,' he said.

'Mornin' Dan,' said his friend. 'What are you so chirpy about this mornin'?'

'Nathin' much… nathin' much,' said Dan O'Donnell. It was a habit of his to repeat things. He watched his friend's eyes return solemnly to the unquestioning headstones, and the smell of decaying leaves and lichen, and he could almost tell intuitively what his friend was thinking. There were a few moments of uncomfortable silence as Dan's original smile was transformed into a frown. He watched silently as his friend took a last long drag and flicked the butt into the entanglement of wet briars and dead flowers that rotted in the corner of the churchyard.

'Y' still miss her; I know y' do,' said Dan eventually.

'A course a do; always will, dammit.' His friend fought back a tear from his disheartened eyes, but his lip and chin quivered. 'She would ha' been twelve now, Dan, with the whole world at her feet. She was bright and funny, and brought Mary and me so much happiness in such a short space of time. Remember her hair? Dan – d' y' remember her hair? Wasn't it the loveliest red y' ever saw?'

'It was, Dec. Surely t' God it was. Like a Red Setter…'

'Remember Dan how she used to sneak up behind a hen and grab its tail feathers and the oul' hen would take off and try to fly and there was the child with this bloody chicken flappin' about and squawkin' in mid air over her head.? 'member?'

'Jeez, a do, Dec... a do.'

'Even the animals loved her. Remember when the cat had her kittens under her bed? Christ, she was a beautiful child,' said Dec, but a look as thick as a mire changed his features. 'But what did I do? I had t' bring strange bloody flowers from America. It was all my fault!' He broke down, his hand over his eyes and his shoulders shuddering.

Dan, like everyone else in Ireland's rural communities, was not given to hugs of comfort and kisses of sympathy – it just wasn't the done thing – but he put his hand awkwardly on his friend's shoulder anyway and patted gently.

'Y' can't keep blamin' yerself, Dec,' he said. 'Accidents happen, and it's just so unfortunate when they happen to an innocent wee girl like... Anna.'

'But it wasn't an accident, Dan. It was me trying to be the big show-off and have all the exotic plants I'd collected from different countries... all lined up along the window sills and in the garden... and all the neighbours lookin' at them and sayin' isn't he the quare fella.'

'Y' weren't t' know... y' weren't t' know. That's life.'

'Don't talk t' me about that's life, Dan. I've just about had m' fill of that's life.' Even as he spoke, Dec's mind was racing back through the years and halting at the memory of little Anna, with her Red Setter hair and skin like porcelain, but with the red blossoms on her lips; beautiful but lethal. Who was to know? Who was to know? Nobody had said anything about the magnificent oleander's deadly poison, and when his daughter had turned pale and sickly and lapsed into unconsciousness they had rushed her to the Letterkenny hospital, but all the stomach pumps, injections, medicines and resuscitations didn't work. His wife, Mary, and he had held their lifeless child in their arms in silence, still with the remains of the fatal blossom on her lips, until the watery autumn sun seemed reluctant to rise over Donegal next morning.

Dec looked round at his friend and for the first time noticed the suitcase in Dan's pudgy hand, and the suit, the collar and tie, and his best flat cap.

'Look at you…' he said, surprised, but glad of the change of thoughts, 'Where are y' goin' all decked out in the whistle an' flute? Holidays are late this year.'

'No, Dec, I'm not goin' on any holiday – wish I was,' said O'Donnell with the dourness of an undertaker. He swallowed hard, then pushed out his chest with a sigh. 'I'm joinin' up, Dec. I'm joinin' the British Army in the mornin'.'

Dec turned slowly once again towards the churchyard.

'So you're finally doin' it are y'? You're takin' the King's shillin'. Well well well. Helpin' the Invader. What did the British ever do for you?' Dec said these things without as much as a glance towards his old friend, who stood fumbling with the handle of the suitcase.

'It's not that, Dec,' said Dan. 'There's bigger things than the turf bogs of Meenacarn y'know. It's about freedom.'

'Freedom? Ha! What about the freedom of your own country? Does that not count?'

'Dec, look. There's a big world over those hills y'know. What's happenin' in the bogs of Ireland is small fry compared to what's goin' on in Germany and Poland… and Russia.' A seething bitterness flashed over Dec's brow, causing little wrinkles to appear at the top of his snipey nose.

'I don't give a damn how many bloody Englishmen the Nazis kill; the more the better as far as I'm concerned. And now my best friend's leavin' his family and friends to go and get slaughtered by Hitler and his henchmen.' Dan O'Donnell was pale and silent. 'I suppose it's true what they say;' Dec added, 'more Irishmen have fought for England than against her, but that alone makes us all look like two-faced eejits. What about the war in your own country?'

'Let's face it, Dec this isn't a war. If war was declared in the real sense of the word the English would finish us in a week.'

'Boy, haven't you become defeatist?

Dan nodded slowly, only adding to the troubled silence between the two friends. Dec turned to face him full on; he had said his piece. Both friends wanted to hug, to kiss even, to run down through the long grass with their homemade willow fishing rods and fish once again on a summer's evening in the Owenamarve river, to build tree huts and watch out to sea for Viking raids, to pinch penny lollies once again from behind Annie the Shop's back. But they both knew they couldn't. Instead they stood in funeral silence, staring at one another. Dan offered his hand. Dec tentatively embraced it.

'Better be headin',' said Dan. 'I've to bus and train it to Belfast before tomorra mornin'… to enlist… y'know.'

It was difficult to separate their hands.

'You've been a good oul' friend, Danny Boy,' said Dec. 'When wee Anna… ten years ago… you were a great help. I'll never forget that.' Dan nodded slowly, turned on his heels and returned back along the Meenacarn Road, excited, yet glued to the hills of his youth. He kept walking, not looking back, until he was merely a well-suited, flat-capped speck lost in the drumlins.

'Well at least I won't have to listen to Dan goin' on about Dec this and Dec that anymore,' said Dec to his wife as he sat down at the fire, tossing his cap carelessly into the corner.

'There always was a bit of the soldier about Dan, wasn't there?' said his wife. 'I remember him at school, always drawing tanks and guns and every stick in his hand was a rifle to him.' Dec lifted a farming journal and scanned it aimlessly. 'He called you Dec all his life, didn't he?' she added, stirring the pot of stew on the range.

'He did. But a nivver had the heart to tell him a hated that silly nickname.'

Mary continued to stir the stew. Later, they sat facing one another at the table in the middle of the room, eating in silence except for the slow ticking of the clock on the mantle, and the occasional craaww from a hen at the half door.

Declan – the name he was christened and the name he preferred – had finished his day's work early so that he would be home before it got dark at five. Besides keeping half-a-dozen milk cows and a couple of scraggy bullocks, a roost of hens and a field of potatoes and cabbages, he did odd jobs about the local farms, like building work, plastering, erecting fences – a general handyman; anything to bring in an extra few shillings to keep bread on the table. His one big regret was that he had never managed to secure full-time farming employment at the Big House in Tramore. In his late teens and early twenties he had believed a good, stable income and fine working conditions were on the cards, thanks in part to his father, who was the head butler at the Big House. All his father had to do was pull the necessary strings and he was in, but one Hallowe'en night his father slipped and fell down the stairs of the Big House and broke his neck. After that, Declan seemed to fall out of favour with the owners and staff at the Big House, really through no fault of his own, and he was consigned to seeking alternative employment where and when he could get it, which wasn't easy at the best of times. Anyway, he now looked upon that episode as the start of his bad luck. From then on, his life seemed to spiral hopelessly downwards; one bad decision after another, fearful of just what lay round the next corner; chronic low self-esteem. If he had the choice between a good decision and a bad, invariably he choose the bad, the useless, the negative.

He was engrossed in these gloomy thoughts when his wife spoke. 'Those carrots are nothing to boast about,' she said. Her husband felt it was such a pathetic observation, and not worth replying to, but she added, 'I forgot to put the salt in until the last minute, then I think I put in too much.'

Since the death of her daughter, Mary had aged forty years in ten. She could never have been described as a vibrant, happy woman anyway – it was just her nature – but she hadn't asked for anything out of life, and now she succumbed to a daily routine of quietly cleaning the range, churning the milk, making the dinner, chasing mice out of the thatch, and knitting Aran pullovers for the craft shop in Dungloe to export to America.

'What do you think of the stew?' she asked quietly. That familiarly venomous look swept over her husband's eyes.

'I think… I think there's more important things in life than your bloody watery stew.' Her eyes dropped, his widened. 'What about that house that's being built right behind us? Is that not more important? Of all the barren acres upon acres of land round about the Snipin' Sweeneys have to build their house so that they're lookin' in through our back door! Ten feet away!' He was livid, because of all the patches of ground he had been left by his father in the will, he was never able to secure the little stretch of grass which ran right up to the back of his own house. It had long since been a thorn in his flesh. He had tried on numerous occasions to purchase it from the owners, who had emigrated to Indiana in the twenties, but was unsuccessful. To him it seemed that some invisible conspiracy of forces barred it. But somehow the Sweeneys had got it, how, he didn't know. And now he looked forward in pessimism to – as he described it – every time I go for a piss at the back door big fat Brenda Sweeney'll have her eyes at the winda.

His outburst over a miserable bowl of stew caused an hour of silence.

By this time of the early evening he would usually have called his dog, Toby, to heel and dandered across the valley to Peter Duffy's, where Barney Boyle and Dan Ward would meet to play cards in Peter's interminably smoky kitchen. But even that pleasure had wearied when, night after night, he went home with less money than when he came out. Surely, given the laws of chance, some small poker bet would fall in his favour and he would go home a penny or two richer. But no. Even the belligerent Barney Boyle had leaned back in his kitchen chair, hugging his cards to his barrel chest and laughed, chuckling to Declan, 'You're def'nit'ly an unlucky sorta divvil the night! Must be that pointy nose a yours!' Declan had shrugged and forced a wry smile, but the observation about his bad luck – too close for comfort – had stung like a thorn.

When he thought about it, his life seemed to have fallen into an unbidden pattern. Most times he was sure that somebody 'up there' was tripping him at every turn, thwarting his plans, spoiling any short-lived pleasure which may come his way, and then sitting back and laughing – just like Barney Boyle had done at the card table – while Declan suffered. He had come to the stage of being sceptical of anything good, fearing an equal, or greater amount of bad just round the corner, waiting to wash the good away like a twig on the shore. If Declan went to the market in Ballybofey to buy a calf, and at the market there were two identical animals, the one which Declan would settle on would be the one that would eventually contract TB, or the red water. Or the choice between two horses; his would turn out lame.

He watched his wife as she stacked turf on the fire. He felt drained.

'Did you bring the milker into the barn for the night?' he asked, turning on the radio to hear any news about the war.

'Oh Jeez,' she breathed, her hand to her mouth. 'I forgot.' Declan jumped up angrily from his chair cursing. He could have easily struck her for her stupidity. As he was pulling on his greatcoat she apologised.

'I'm forgetting everything these days… I don't know what's got into my head…' Declan called the dog from the barn and turned to his wife.

'Forgot this, forgot that… that's all a hear. Have you seen the size of your backside recently? You're obviously not forgetting t' eat!' And with that he flattened the cap on his head and raged off.

She was sitting in the gloom knitting when he got home half an hour later. Tick. Knit one. Tock. Purl one. Tick. Knit one. Tock. Purl one. He sat down, but he was fidgety. He wrung his cap in his hands and tapped his foot to a nervous, silent tune.

'Meery,' he said eventually. 'I just don't know anymore.' She kept her head down; her eyes were red with having wept since he left. 'I can honestly say with my hand on my heart that I've always tried to do the right thing…'

'I know y' have…' she said.

'But it seems that this black cloud just won't go away no matter what. I forget the last time I made a right decision or did the right thing. It's as if I'm always fightin' against something; either fate or people. I don't know if I can do this any more.' With that he stood up, adjusted his braces over his shoulders, and put on his cap. His wife watched him with resigned eyes. He put on his coat and lifted the shotgun down from its hide in the thatch above the front door. Without a word he was swallowed up by the darkness, and in her heart she knew that this was the last time she'd see him.

He made his way down to the river, through the front garden once pretty but now bereft of flowers, walking through the long damp grass that whipped and wet his legs. A dog's bark echoed over a far hillside; a hillside now only slightly darker than the starry sky. He sat on a dry rock and listened to the music of the river over the cold stones, gurgling and racing on its way to the Atlantic. He felt he was going to burst, like a bad boil on the back of his neck. When he considered his life it seemed now like one long trial, a matrix of misfortune and he wished – God, he only wished – he knew what he had done to deserve it.

A rustling of a large creature in the fanin behind him startled him so much that he almost lost his seating and couped into the freezing river. He instinctively let out a curse, and in the blue light of the moon he saw two young deer, having made a grazing expedition down from the hills, chomping only feet away. He watched their silvery backs for a good ten minutes until they were once again engulfed in the shadows of bushes cast by the moon. Their beauty and rawness cheered his spirits slightly. He flicked the last of his cigarette into the river, hissing, and made the climb with cold-stiffened muscles back up to the house, shivering in the chill.

Mary had gone on to bed, at least he thought, so he didn't call to check where she was before he blew out the lamp. He went out to settle the cow and give the dog its crust when he found his wife – Mary Ann Quish – hanging by her neck from a rafter in the barn.

MY HOMETOWN

BOYS A DEAR, IT'S BEEN MANY A YEAR since I walked these roads; twenty-five, maybe even thirty, since I even set foot in my hometown. When I say *town*, the place isn't, nor never has officially been a town. It only ever had the population of a village, but for some reason it was never referred to by its inhabitants as a village. I can't remember ever hearing the word village mentioned. Maybe it was because the word village sounded too English, too high-faluting, too nice for the simple, hard-working, no frills folk back then. And yet nowadays, from afar, I see in the papers, and when I enquire about the old place I notice it called village quite a lot, mostly by blow-ins, the English, and zealous traders and business people who probably think that village sounds more quaint, more nursery rhyme, in keeping with their new vision of how they want to promote and define it for tourists and investment. But to me it will always be a town, for better or worse.

I have returned this morning for a dander through the old haunts, to reminisce, to bring myself up to date with the changes, and also because I miss the place. Like swallows returning through dangerous skies from the heat of Africa, there must be some special inbred genetic magnet in all living things, forever pulling us back to the spot where we first breathed earthly air.

I park beside the bank, and straightening my woolly hat and giving a quick check in the rear-view mirror to make sure I haven't left morsels of Corn Flakes on my chin, I pinch my cheeks to bring some colour to my winter pallor. I step out into a nippy Sunday morning. Ten o'clock and I'd long since forgotten how loudly the church bells toll. A patchy covering of snow skulks at the edges of footpaths, and shelters in behind cold walls and exposed earth. My fingers and kneecaps respond instantly to the chill biting through to my bones and I think that when I last played in this street in the big snowfall of '63 I probably never even felt the cold. Now, I'm glad I brought gloves and scarf with me.

The old bank could do with a lick of paint. It's a wonder the town's new traders' committee – formed to oversee that everything in the town looks right – hasn't paid a wee visit to the manager and pointed out the flaky paintwork and crumbling window frames… it's not becoming of the village's image… for tourists and the like… investment… development… for the betterment of the community… and all that. I don't recall the bank's façade being in such poor state on the day, about forty years ago – I was eight or nine – when I walked up the street from our house in the middle of the town and proudly opened my first savings account with one shilling. I was now a man of means. Think of the interest! I signed on a dotted line – babyish it must have been – at the bottom of the form and the manager, a grey-haired man in a grey suit with the bank's shiny grey walls as a backdrop held the form admiringly at arm's length and said that my handwriting was indeed beautiful and that you don't see writing like that anymore. He studied it like an art critic. Calling a cashier over he asked for her opinion. 'Beautiful,' she agreed. I was pleased, and, beaming with pride couldn't wait until I'd saved another shilling. I smile to myself when I realise that I haven't much more than a shilling in my account forty years later!

The Primary School. Well well well. It's being demolished. It was only built in the late fifties, a lovely, simple white building with five classrooms and a principal's office. Come to think of it – and I haven't done until now – I must have been one its first pupils; one who began in P1 and went right through to P7. And now, because of the ever-mushrooming rampant population the old place must succumb to a bigger, more monstrous construction, a thing the size of two aircraft hangars and just as bland being hastily erected in the adjoining playing fields. It just doesn't seem right that the old school had such a short life span – for a building that is. All those builders; block upon block, brick upon brick, makers of joists and window frames and doors, joiners, plumbers, electricians, plasterers, makers of blackboards and desks, layers of parquet floors, all working tirelessly for the education of the country's youngsters, who, come a measly forty-five years later will pull the craftsmens' work asunder without remorse. Headmasters, teachers, (my first official boyhood crush was on my P3 teacher, who was the only woman I knew then who sported a Beatle fringe) the caretaker, dinner ladies, the rhythmic slapping of skipping ropes on the pavement, girls giggling, *if y' step on a spider you'll marry a gypsy*, working out what age we will all be in the year 2000, boasting that you'd filled your big blue League of Pity Easter egg and you should get an enamel badge this year, trying to get Margaret Mayne to climb a tree so we could catch a glimpse of what colour her pants were, a boy scores a goal on the tarmac pitch; another Stanley Matthews in the making. The playground empties suddenly and mysteriously of boys. Word has gone about that Sharon Thompson is in the headmaster's store and is showing *everything* for 2d a go! Margaret Mayne is swiftly forgotten up the tree as we dash across the playground, rummaging in our pockets for the required fee.

And even the playing fields. They were once a big, unkempt acre or two with two mature sycamores and a couple of straggly ponies grazing indifferently. I would practise throwing my boomerang in there; the nearest open space to our house in the street where there was less chance of breaking a window. I became quite an expert with the Australian weapon, most times being able to catch it when it returned, and the better I got the fewer windows I broke. Then one day tractors and bulldozers burst through the hedge and trampled over the field. They began ripping the sods and knocking down the two sycamores. We watched the grim proceedings from our P5 classroom. The red clay was dug to some unearthly depth and tons and tons of stones rattled from the backs of lorries, changing the landscape forever. The headmaster, watching with us, told us that the stones were for drainage and that the two new football pitches would never flood. It was state-of-the-art engineering.

The opening night was a balmy summer evening with Margaret Mayne sitting dangling her legs prettily over the new wall, just above the *Playing Fields* sign. A silver band marched about and a marquee sold drinks and buns. A 5-a-side competition had been organised to celebrate the opening and teams from as far away as Lisburn – five miles away – arrived in minibuses and dads' cars. Our team, which didn't make it to the second round, were called The Maggots. The organiser chastised us and told us that we should've taken the tournament more seriously.

I pass the estate of houses to where we moved in the sixties, my father having sold the wee house in the town for six hundred pounds. The new house seemed like a mansion, and the gardens front and rear were a real novelty. The air is still chilly as I climb the hill. My dad told me once that where the estate is now, and precisely where our new house stands there was once a football pitch – the home ground of Downshire FC – and beside the pitch ran a long blackthorn hedge, a sort of tall rugged terrace which provided only scanty shelter for the ten or fifteen supporters huddled together on a wet Saturday afternoon with icy gusts blowing up the hill and stinging their ears. *Come on the Downshire!* In the summer, with his baby daughter perched on his broad shoulders he complained that the midgees from that hedge *would've ate the neck a y'.*

I leave the town behind, with the high demesne wall of the forest park at my shoulder. A new development of houses (they're not called estates any more in keeping with the new affluence) that may have come straight from a Dickens novel have spawned over once ploughed and grazed fields, and the hedge in which Joe Gillespie claims he once saw a ghost, or a banshee, or felt some unnatural influence, is gone; the site of the spooky appearance now part of some unsuspecting family's back garden.

These roads were once black with people walking out on Sunday evenings, in all weathers. Lovers, families, old couples breathing the fresh, unslurried air, the village idiots and some chronic alcoholics shuffling along, and it was difficult to walk twenty yards without meeting someone you knew. A gossip, a moan about the weather and the Labour government (I mind the time…), while the children jumped from foot to foot with impatience to get on with the walk and get home to watch Fireball XL5. Walking out on Sundays by the masses died out, indeed, to witness the obesity of people nowadays it would seem that walking, or any sort of physical activity at all, has died out altogether.

Roads became dangerous, borne out by a proliferation of memorials of crosses and cellophane wrapped flowers on every country road. In the dark, along unlit rural roads and lanes, if two cars meet, I have noticed there is a definite black spot, an unlit tunnel, to the left, beside the kerb immediately in front of each car. It is in this dark spot of death that most pedestrians, I assume, meet their end. I've often thought that maybe a second lamp, a light that emits a penetrative beam – a ray – rather than a glow should be fitted beside the nearside light of all cars that would pierce the darkness and maybe save lives… who knows?

My father came to hate walking along here. He would complain, as the roads got busier and busier, that if you're not careful you could easily get a whack on the back of the head with a lorry's wing mirror.

'Have y' seen how far the wing mirrors stick out nowadays?' he would grumble. 'The other day a white van flew past me so close he damn near took the kep off m' head!'

The old green gate into the forest is still the same; awkward and ugly and stiff. The small corrugated iron door is only big enough for a leprechaun to pass through without bending down. For all other normally statured individuals getting into the forest grounds can be a harrowing experience, with, at the very least, trying to prevent the razor-sharp edges of the tin doorway slicing your hand. I'm sure many a coat, or new pullover, or pair of tights has been viciously unravelled at this spot. It's a wonder that the prosperous new community hasn't complained, and while you're at it, why not knock down part of the hundred-and-fifty year old wall down and make a car park?

Joggers. Three joggers jogging in English accents, decked out in the finest and most expensive jogging gear, no doubt. A young woman walks my way, walking her dog. There's no-one else on this short stretch of pathway so she hurriedly rummages in her handbag and brings out her mobile phone and pretends to be having this deep conversation with someone. It's an old ruse, I know, but I understand. A flasher has been frequenting these paths lately, and the joke about town is that there are more single women taking walks in the forest than ever before. One elderly lady was heard to boast that if he flashed at her she'd hit it with her umbrella. The girl's overweight black Labrador waddles up to me and sniffs my knee, leaving its slobbers all over my trouser leg. It's wagging its tail, but even so, if it jumps up on me I am determined to launch my boot into its balls. Luckily for him, he splutters off and reluctantly returns to the girl, who has been frantically screaming, 'Tarquin! Tarquin! Come here this moment Tarky old boy!'

These dank and dripping dark trees – firs, cedars, oaks – that now colonnade the walkways were once all cut down. The forest was flattened. The place looked like a nuclear disaster site for years; dead tree trunks like a box of spilled matches. It was sad, but the timber was probably needed elsewhere; that's what it was grown for in the first place. We were angry and rebellious because now we had nowhere to build our hideouts. But indomitable nature soon proliferated again and the forest, slowly and surely, over a number of years, returned to its original lusciousness.

More sprightly walkers. Morn-eeng! More terriers with little tinkling bells on their collars.

It may have been Charlie Witherspoon in the late sixties on Scene Around Six, sitting like a gnome on a bough jutting out into the lake, extolling the sites and rustic sounds of this quaint little village lost in County Down. Because at first there was a slow, almost imperceptible trickle of strangers on a Sunday afternoon, and then a great tsunami of tourists and picnickers and anglers and litter and dog crap. I blame Charlie, anyway. We hated to watch as our hidden paths and trails were opened and gravelled and signposted. Bushes and trees were hacked down for wheelchair access and better views of the lake and church, and everywhere walkers and their dogs swarmed in their hundreds. A brand new car park boasted a smelly *Dog Fouling Area* (I ask y' … did y' ever hear the like of it?), and instead of bream and roach in the lake it was restocked with the best of trout for fly fishers and the RUC Angling Club.

We made a raft once, out of about twenty logs purloined from the Forestry Commission office, and eight empty oil barrels tied to the hull with baler twine. She proved seaworthy enough when tested amongst the bulrushes, so four of us set sail for the little uninhabited island in the middle of the lake, using long poles to push her along. Halfway out we took stock. 'Can anybody swim?' one of the four ventured to ask. There were shrugs of negativity all round. Then we got scared. The water got choppy and a cloud covered the sun. The water turned leaden and unfriendly as we pushed like the clappers to get to the island before somebody fell overboard, stunned by the sudden realisation that if one of us were to fall in there would be no-one diving in to save him. As we hit the shore one of the philosophers in the group declared, 'This is crazy! That's how people get drowned!' And we all began fearing the return journey. But while we were there we dug a small hole in the muddy, root-entangled ground and buried a jam jar containing a scrap of paper with our names, the date, what age each of us was, and a shiny new two-pence piece. Our return journey was uneventful – in that nobody drowned – but we were all a bit nervous and glad to reach yon farther shore. We boasted of our exploits to our land-lubber friends and two days later David Mackie, with unrestrained devilment goaded us with the sombre news that he and his gang had found our raft moored in the rushes and they, too, had sailed to the island. 'We found your money, too!' he bragged.

We used to call this patch of ground beside the water's edge the Mossy. At one time the moss was so thick and lush here it resembled a soft, green carpet sweeping down to the lapping lake. My sisters trilled their Easter eggs down the gently sloping Mossy on their Easter picnics as Mum and Dad no doubt reclined on a tartan rug with sandwiches and biscuits and a flask of sugary tea. I vaguely remember the spongy greenness under my chubby feet, but soon the narrow trail had been widened for prams and tricycles and easy access for visitors, and the moss eventually got worn away. I see it's all gone now, and so are the rhododendrons wherein as lads we hid and sipped our first cans of warm Guinness on our summer holidays. Our young stomachs, repulsed by the smoky black fluid, hurled it back up again over the bushes. No-one could face the fourth can so we buried it in the ground behind the rhododendrons for safe keeping. We promised we'd come back the next day and finish it off, brave warriors that we were, but never did. Life passed by, but I'm sure that that same unopened can still lies buried in the ground, somewhere near to where I now stand.

The water from the lake laps against old tree stumps that jut out like rotten teeth over the lake, used for the last forty years by fishermen to get that extra few feet into the water. There's a great view from here of the Fort and the Fort field. They say King Billy slept in the fort one night on his march to the Boyne, but my mind turns to lustier things as I recall the tentative, stunted walks with a new girlfriend, hand in nervous hand, running out of things to say and thanking King Billy from the bottom of my heart that even three hundred years after his victorious triumph he helps me out and gives me something to talk about.

'Did he really?' she says, impressed.

'They say he tied his white horse to that tree over there...' And when I feel she is tiring of the history lesson I go in for the kill, something I know will amaze and astound her: 'We made a raft once...'

The wooden benches have yellow graffiti (Marco+Death) sprayed on them. Fag butts mingle in the gravel. Beer cans bent and floating. It was such invasion by strangers and aliens that forced us to form our very own army of resistance in the seventies. It wasn't an actual army as such; just five or six boys with home-made bows and arrows who wanted passionately to keep the forest secret and for the exclusive use of people from the town... the way it had always been. We made the best bows we could out of long lengths hewn from the yew trees in the churchyard. The arrows of willow were flighted with feathers plucked from dead crows we found in the undergrowth and, with roughly camouflaged clothes of headbands and shirts and beige cords we were a regular wee tribe of Apache braves, preserving the sanctity of our homelands – and prepared to fight for it.

We would secret ourselves in the bushes along various points on the pathways, pretending to whistle to each other in code, mimicking bird sounds, but not one of us having the foggiest notion about what the other ones were whistling about. And when an unsuspecting young family, or two lovers, or a middle-aged couple strolled by for their Saturday or Sunday afternoon picnic we showered them with arrows from all directions accompanied with tribal screams of 'Go home!' and 'Get out of our park!' and 'Away back to Belfast y' buggers!' Once I broke cover from the greenery of a dense rhododendron and, standing defiantly in the middle of the path fired an arrow in the direction of three walkers. (I had first checked that they were walking away from me.) The arrow shot through the air, peppered by spots of sunlight in its long, satisfying trajectory, making a little whoosh sound as it went, and lodged itself in the calf of one of the men. Before he had time to give out a cry of pain the five of us had scarpered for cover and were frantically scrambling over ferns and fallen trees with our hearts – well, mine anyway – pumping hard with fear of repercussion. I could've killed him. I could've punctured his brain with that bloody arrow. So much for our fight for freedom. The tribe dispersed soon after that scare – we hadn't meant to hurt anyone – and anyway, we grew up and wised up, and the cavalry and the dudes from the East took over our lands.

Another fenced-off patch of dead grass. DOG FOULING AREA – NO PEDESTRIANS. I question the mentality of any pedestrian who would walk through a dog fouling area, or is it supposed to mean that no pedestrians are permitted to foul in that area?

Forty swans and cygnets, graceful and snobbish, expectant of crumbs. I should have brought the half loaf that was lying on the kitchen table after breakfast this morning, but I never thought. The reflection of the blindingly bright morning sun on the surface of the lake pierces my eyes; the swans dull in comparison.

A car park full of Beemers, Jeeps, Volvos. A 911 crouches in the shady corner.

Isn't it strange to think that those people who have bought homes and built their mansions and settled here recently and altered the town out of all recognition will be the ones who, come fifty years' time, will bemoan the changes forced upon them by an even newer wave of blow-ins? They – the new ones now – will be the old people of the town one day. But I take hope. Everything has to change, eventually. Things wear out, people's attitudes change with the times. New things come, old things go, but as long as the heart of a community stays positive, and there exists a willingness and a drive by its inhabitants to preserve its soul, then those who have gone before can rest assured, knowing that their community lives on in compassionate hands.

This hill, the main street, at one time I thought was almost insurmountable. It was a hill where lorries jack-knifed and cars lost control on the ice and where your lungs burned when you were crazy enough to cycle up it. But now it seems – miraculously – almost flat.

A man, about the same age as I, walks his bicycle up the hill, slightly out of breath.

'Mornin',' I say.

'Hiya,' he answers. It sounds strange. It sounds strange to hear an adult with a beard and grey hair and an old black bike offer such a teenage greeting. Sometimes I would tend to say Hiya, just as he did, but up until this minute I believed it to be the vocabulary of a younger generation, and someone like myself saying it sounds just like what it is; an old bugger trying to stay in his youth, like wearing trainers or dying your hair. But now that I've heard it from another's lips I am convinced it doesn't sound too contrived so I'll continue to use it at will.

'Hiya,' I say to a large-breasted woman embracing the morning sun at her front door.

'Fresh morning,' she says. I smile to her and walk on.

I pass the Post Office. Well, it's not the Post Office anymore. At one time it was the Post Office, General Hardware Store, Taxi Rank and Undertaker's. Anything from a needle to a coffin. *It's not the coughin' that carries you off; it's the coffin they carry you off in.* It looks as if it's a boutique or something now, but my mind races back to one day as I was in the Post Office buying a stamp and posting a letter for my mother when a man and a woman – both American tourists – came in. They were asking old Ned the Postmaster for directions.

'Howdy... we're lookin' for a place by the name of —' I can't remember where he asked for, but as I stood at the counter licking my stamp and listening to the broad, strange accents, old Ned came from his office and enquired, 'Where did y' say?' The big Yank repeated , clumsily unfolding his road map of Ireland. It would remind you of the first meeting of John Wayne and Barry Fitzgerald in The Quiet Man; Ned, with his dusty black suit and collarless shirt perfectly cast as the old matchmaker.

'No,' said Ned, scratching his chin. 'It doesn't ring a bell...'

'It doesn't what?' quizzed the flummoxed Yank.

'...doesn't ring a bell...' Ned repeated, unaware that something had been lost in translation.

'There's no mention of a bell on the map...' the Yank added, turning to his equally baffled wife. I posted my Mum's letter and left before I burst out laughing.

I approach the little terrace house in the street where my family and I were all born, bred and buttered. Right in the middle of the town. Through that window, in that room overlooking the street is where I made my grand entrance into the world, no doubt bawling and yelling with the frown lines on my forehead already formed.

The Sunday school, and at one time the local school, was held in a large building directly across the street. The body of the school was one enormous hall with its classes of differing age groups forming little half circles at the walls; five or six students facing in towards the teacher. Then, come eleven o'clock on a Sunday morning we sang a hymn, said a prayer with eyes half open, and at Amen we rushed out the door to get home, where we met up with our parents who had on their best Sunday clothes, ready for church. It was the same ritual every Sunday with me, until one Sunday in particular. When the collection was being taken – the plate, or basket, being graciously carried round the classes by the teachers' favourites – it came to my class, at the end of the hall furthest away from the door. But when I put my hand deep into my shorts' pocket I found to my horror that I had forgotten my sixpence collection. No matter how much I dug into the corners of my pockets, front and back, there was nothing there except the hanky my mum had given me that morning. I was too numb to speak. I squirmed on my fold-up chair. The teacher, an officious ginger-haired do-gooder, glared at me. 'Where's your money?'

'I've… I've forgot it,' I stammered. A reasonable solution, I would've thought – and still do – would've been to call me a forgetful blockhead and that I'd forget my own head if it wasn't screwed on, but make sure you bring double amount next week. But no. Not Mister Good Samaritan. The old rascal knew I lived just across the street.

'Okay then,' he said sternly in his best QUB accent. 'Go and get it.' I stared back, hoping against hope he was only joking. But his bulging, serious rat eyes told me he wasn't. Had this happened in my later years I would've told him to wise up, take a reality pill, chill man, I'll bring it next week, don't get your knickers in a twist. But then, as a seven-year-old, with His Nibs scowling down at me, my stomach churning, the weight and power of unquestionable religious authority strangling me, feeling the eyes and embarrassed silence of the class drill into me, I was humiliated, abused, scared. 'Go on,' he ordered.

One of the longest walks I've ever had to endure in my life was the one I made down the length of that hall on that sunny God fearing, Love Thy Neighbour Sunday. Now fifty eyes were on me, whispering and wondering why Jim Burrows was being sent home. My legs, leaden with mortification, almost buckled below me. I somehow got out the front door into the stifle-free air and burst out crying. I stood at the front gates for a moment or two trying to contain myself before facing Dad. I was still sobbing when I told him the story.

'You'll be taking no bloody sixpence to that man this morning,' my dad said with angry authority. '…and him supposed to be a Christian.' And with Dad's tender support and understanding suddenly the world was all right again. I never had to go back to Sunday school after that. All the factors had conspired to ensure, from that moment onwards, my slow, but definite, downward spiral to atheism.

I can see my car. I've walked in a sort of circle, right round the outskirts of the town and hardly saw a one. As a boy I could have named every family in this street: the Jenkins, the Beeches, the Halls, the McCarthys, the Sleators, the Currys, the Robinsons… all gone now. You could've walked the length of this street, and, I suppose, every other street in every other part of the country and, given the right time of day, told what each family was having for dinner. In the days before extractor fans, microwaves, eating out and carry-outs, the delicious mouth-watering whiffs of each family's cooking tumbled out the front door and onto the street, warming you on a cold day, making you jealous, stirring your soul.

'The Sleators are havin' mince and onions tonight,' I would announce to Mum as she slaved away thanklessly at a big pot of steaming potatoes in the dark scullery, throwing my schoolbag into the cubby hole under the stairs. 'Could we have mince and onions? It's been donkeys since we had mince and onions! Please!' My mouth had gushed saliva since I first stepped past the Sleators' front door. The Jenkins were having homemade vegetable and chicken soup. The steam from champ and sausages puffed out from the Robinsons' pokey scullery. The Halls were having fish.

I reach my car, my head nauseous with memories. The air is clear and sharp. No smells of dinners anymore. There's only one smell now: the smell of progress.

A PROCESS
OF ELIMINATION

SOME THINGS IN LIFE JUST SEEM TO CREEP UP ON YOU, like when you realise you've reached the age when, if you should plant a tree, you'll never see it fully grown. Or that scary day when your son becomes taller than you, so that you can't whack him the same as you once did, or when your baby daughter suddenly and without warning becomes the age when she herself could have a daughter.

It was one such unnoticed time when the man from Dromore realised with grim despair that he hadn't 'visited the outhouse' (if you know what I mean) for nearly a week. It wasn't like him. You could've set your watch by his bowels. All his life he'd been as regular as a regiment, invariably rolling the day's News Letter under his arm at o-nine-thirty hours, after his morning mouthful, and marching valiantly down the garden path to the tarred outhouse at the bottom of the garden. All the other farms in the area had had mains water installed years ago, but he wouldn't have given up his dry toilet for anything. He would spend a good ten minutes scanning the big pages; them rustling in the tiny room and the smell of honeysuckle wafting through the vent. It was his own few minutes of private bliss, and then the moment of release was one of sublime inspiration, almost divine, a liberation of mind and waste. It was in fond remembrance of such euphoria that shocked him into wondering how such perfection had gone unnoticed for almost a week.

But now the situation was desperate. When he became conscious that he hadn't enjoyed a full, satisfying evacuation for so long it panicked him. It was like whenever you find you've run out of heating oil, or the boiler breaks down, the house seems instantly colder. Or when you touch a radiator, expecting it to be warm, but even though it's only turned off and cold, it feels frozen.

He had to confess to his wife. 'My bowels hasn't moved for nearly a week,' he said, kicking a Rhode Island Red out of the kitchen in frustration.

'I'll make you a nice apple and rhubarb tart,' said his wife brightly. 'That'll shift y'. Have y' been aytin' your apple every day?' The man's head dropped in guilty silence. He hadn't. Even though his good lady left a beautiful bowl of fruit on the sideboard as a permanent feature, keeping it well stocked up with apples, oranges, plums in season, and bananas, he admitted he hadn't partaken of late. He reasoned that he'd been too busy; there was calving going on, the collie had been sick and he'd had to drive the sheep himself; a wearisome practice of throwing carefully aimed stones and shouting at the senseless beasts.

The apple and rhubarb tart, and indeed the prune juice, grapes, concentrated pure orange juice, bran bread and castor oil didn't work either, and after two weeks the man from Dromore looked pregnant and awkward on his feet.

'What in the name of Jaysus amma goin' to do?' moaned the man from Dromore to the old man in the pub the next Friday night. At one time old men had a standard dress code: black suit with waistcoat, flat cap and hob-nail boots. But now the dress for old men was more likely to be a light grey suit from Oxfam, dirty trainers and a baseball cap. But the man in the pub wasn't a good man to confide in either; he had a bad stomach at the best of times, even to the point of feeling sick if he happened to see the inside of a sausage roll. He complained that he'd had a ulster in his stomach most of his life. 'I feel like a mobile compost heap,' the man from Dromore confided.

'Do y' know the wife?' he asked after gazing at the back of a big-boned woman standing at the bar waiting to be served. The look of her nearly scared him. She had skin-tight leggings which accentuated her substantial curves. She bore the unfortunate feature of possessing love-handles which were as big and as plump and bulbous as her already ample buttocks so that she appeared as if she was carrying a television set down the back of her trousers.

'The wife? Now who might that be?' asked the man in the pub.

'She's the wee fat wummin with a hump on her back…'

'Ach sure a know her now. Why?'

'Well, she's been feedin' me all the roughage and bran o' the day. It's as if she's feedin' a damned horse. I might as well be out grazin' in the field.'

'Have y' tried the Sirrpa Figs?'

'Every damn bloody thing I've tried. Nothin'll budge it. All she does is chastise me that I haven't been aytin' her apple every day.'

'…keeps the doctor away, they say.' said the man in the pub smugly, and then added without blinking an eyelid, 'Imagine goin' home a shillin' short in your wages to thon thing at the bar…'

The man in the pub was pensive. There was a long silence as he lit his pipe and pushed his John Deere baseball cap back, exposing a pink forehead. He took a long puff, puffing the blue smoke into the air. The man from Dromore was silent. He thought the man in the pub was still fantasising about the horse at the bar. The silage smell of the tobacco smoke caught his throat. He coughed violently, but took a long swallow of his beer and that seemed to settle him. The man in the pub, when he saw that the other had calmed down, asked a strange question: 'Have y' ever heard of the Elimination Paradox?' It was almost whispered, like a Masonic greeting, or two friends meeting at a funeral.

'The… what?' asked the man from Dromore. He couldn't remember a time in his life when he'd heard two such grand and confusing words at all, never mind both in the same sentence on the same day.

'The Elimination Paradox,' the other said, more slowly this time, looking secretive, almost shiftily, conspiratorially covering his mouth.

'The Elim—?'

'Keep it down! Keep it down!' the other scolded. 'This is big stuff y'know. Y'don't want the world and his wife to know about it!' The man from Dromore felt small and disregarded, like when you're trying to tell somebody something but they're more interested in what's on TV.

'Nivver heard of it,' he whispered.

'Gettis a pint and we'll talk about it.'

The man from Dromore was all ears; he had an ear on his forehead, one on his cheek, two at the back of his head and twenty or thirty over his body. Well, he didn't really, but he was so absorbed in what the man in the pub had to say he felt he had ears everywhere.

'The Elimination Paradox,' the man went on, reminding the man from Dromore of Patrick Moore on the Sky at Night, 'can only be administered in the direst of circumstances. Unless a body is totally and irreversibly compacted, without any hope of alleviation will the Wise Old Woman from the Waters even consider a remedy. Understand?'

'I understand… sort of. But one thing I do know is that I am totally and irreversibly compacted… and have been for two long weeks.'

'Well then. I have here in my wallet the name of a man who can put you in touch with…' The man in the pub paused, patting the wallet which was in the inside pocket of his jacket. It became a very pregnant pause. Not only pregnant; now it was long overdue. The man from Dromore waited with bated anticipation, but the man in the pub had suddenly turned a greyish, clammy green. He gasped. He stuttered something while clenching his chest. At first the man from Dromore smirked when he thought it was all a jolly jape.

'Come on,' he said, on the cusp of bursting out laughing, 'stop acting the Clampett.' Just then the other man's head slumped onto the table with a deathly thud, spilling his drink over the both of them, and attracting the attention of everybody in the bar, including the big girl with the square backside.

The man from Dromore still had the helpless look of an imbecile on his face when the big girl rushed over to help, her enormous breasts swaying like two sows being drowned in a barrel. Within seconds she had taken charge of the situation and had loosened the dying man's collar and tie and was administering first aid with admirable tenacity. 'I'm a nurse,' she said confidently between kisses of life.

'Very nice,' said the man from Dromore. She pumped at his chest. It was a sight to behold.

'I'm a sister at the Lagan Valium Hospital,' she said, laughing and swaying.

'I'm from Dromore,' he said, but his head was in two or three places at the same time. One half of his brain was in a state of panic that his mentor had just died a violent and sickening death in the pub beside him while on the brink of parting with much needed information. Another part of his mind was wondering devilishly yet guiltily on how he could get the slip of paper out of the dead man's wallet without an ensuing conviction for robbery of the dead, and the third half of his brain was transfixed on the stretched gap between the button holes of the nurse's overworked blouse and the mammoth mammaries juggling with each puff; two great udders in danger of popping about three or four buttons into oblivion at any second.

'I think he's gone,' she said eventually, a swathe of perspiration shining on her upper lip. 'I'm sorry.' An ambulance siren screamed nearby, coming in their direction.

The man from Dromore put his arm round the dead shoulders of his friend and confidant. Everybody in the pub was touched at his affection for his fallen comrade. He felt about and soon his hand rested on the corpse's wallet in his inside pocket. Now or never. 'Thanks, old friend,' he whispered into the dead man's hairy ear, 'great will be your reward in heaven.'

Outside, as everyone waited for the mortuary van to arrive, the man from Dromore opened the crumpled note. He naively expected the note to be clear cut and exact, something like: Wise Old Woman of the Waters, 5 Main Street, Gurtymadden, County Down, or some such easily found address. But instead, written on the back of a bus ticket was: Old Conal – Knocknashee. But I thought it was an old woman I was looking for, the man from Dromore thought to himself. This old man, Conal, must be part of a jigsaw that leads to the Wise Old Woman of the Waters.

The Dromore man – the one with the bloated stomach and ghostly pallor – knew of only one Knocknashee, and it was in the back end of nowhere in the middle of county somewhere. He pulled on his bicycle clips and straightened his cap and cycled southwards, obtaining vague and sometimes downright misleading directions from strangely strange strangers on the way.

'Knocknashee is it you're lookin'?' screeched one old turf-faced hag, whacking a cow with the flat of her hand. 'Go on! Y'baste y'!' she admonished, and without turning she asked, 'Now why would a lost soul as yerself be a-lookin' to go to Knocknashee? Sure it's only a wee hill, no bigger than a bishop's bum!' She screeched her screech again and amid slobbers and saliva and scratching she pointed him like a lost child in the rough direction of Knocknashee. He plundered on, constipated and forlorn.

He stopped with a young man; an educated, eccentric-looking sort of chap.

'Am a near a place called Knocknashee?' the bound-up man asked.

'Knocknashee. Now let me see…' He tapped his chin the way only English people do. After what seemed like donkeys the educated man said, much to the surprise of the other, 'I conjecture there's only one reason you wish to visit the aforementioned location. And only one certain personage you intend to visit… am I right?'

'W w w w well,' stuttered the man from Dromore. 'You could be right. But it's for personal reasons.'

'I knew it!' said the other, now displaying an annoying tic of patting the side of his chin three times, then his forehead, all in one swift movement while his eyes rolled skyward. The man from Dromore was fascinated. 'Do you see that hill over there?' He did his tic thing again and pointed to a hill with a rugged outcrop dotted with sheep. 'That's Knocknashee, my man, and the man you're looking for resides at that very location.' As he got more excited the tic got worse, to the point when the man from Dromore thought the man was going to swat himself to death.

The man from Dromore was relieved. No, not relieved in a way pertaining to the subject of this story; just relieved in his mind. 'Thank you,' he said. 'Thank you very much.' He threw his leg over his bicycle and was off again, hoping that his journey was at last coming to a close.

'Don't mention it old chap,' the man shouted after him. 'But be careful. With Old Conal you could get more than you bargained for! Like when you're at the toilet and your finger goes through the roll!' He laughed, did a few swats at his chin and forehead and skipped off on his way. 'Good luck!' he shouted, the breeze whisking his words into oblivion. He waved his hand in the air without looking back.

Old Conal had a fire lit at the door of his craggy cave and was boiling water in a big, soot-blackened pot, while a giant Irish Wolfhound sniffed lazily about.

'Finnegan!' he shouted at the dog, and it swaggered a confident swagger over to his master and lay down at his feet. Then he turned his attention to the stranger.

'Who sent y'?' he barked from under a dark, suspicious frown. Then, before the man from Dromore had a chance to open his mouth, 'Who toul' y' where til find me? Who are y'? Are y' from the government? If y' are, then you've wasted your time climbing up here…'

'No, blast y'! I'm not from any government,' the man from Dromore said. The dog gave a low growl, unhappy at the stranger's raised tone.

'Have y' any hidden microphones?'

'No, I don't have any damn hidden microphones or whatever y' call them. Y' can search me if y' want.'

'What's the point,' said Old Conal, tetchily tugging at his beard and straightening some stray strands of straggly, greasy hair. He thought for a moment and then, 'Are y' a spy from the Military then?'

'No spy, either.'

'Then what do y' want with me?' He sat down on a flat granite rock and spat into the fire. It sizzled nicely. After a long pause, during which time both men sat and took the time to watch a pair of buzzards hovering majestically in the warm air currents over Knocknashee, the man from Dromore said, 'I was given your name by a man in Belfast (he lied) who said you could help me in my, a, predicament. I've biked, walked, bussed, trained, and climbed mountains to find you. Can you help a poor soul in need?'

Old Conal was pensive. The suspiciousness had left him. He began to warm to the stranger.

'I take it you haven't shit in weeks?' He laughed.

'Well, yes. I suppose you could call it that.'

'Well, come over here,' said Old Conal. The man from Dromore shifted to a new rock. The water in the cauldron began to boil.

'Keep quiet now,' Old Conal said, looking about him, over his shoulder, down the hill, furtive and nervous. The man from Dromore felt that this was it; he was at last going to enjoy relief. Old Conal put his finger up to his lips to emphasise silence, and then, when only the hush of the hills was in their ears, he whispered, 'They're listenin' to us now y'know.' The other man glanced over his own shoulder.

'Who?' he whispered.

'The agents,' he mouthed. 'Government agents.'

The disconsolate Dromore man wondered why in the name of Jesus and Mary would anybody want to listen in to a conversation in the middle of nowhere about the needs of one man to go to the toilet.

'What agents?' he asked.

'They're watching our every move. Monitoring us from their satellites out in space. The buggers are controlling everything we do, everything we see, everything we look at. I got fed up with their games, and that's why I'm here.' He seemed pleased with himself.

'But all I want is a cure for…'

'I know, I know,' said Old Conal, 'but listen til me first.' The Dromore man's curiosity was killing him.

'What makes y' think we're bein' watched?

'Och, sure it's obvious! Do y' not read the papers? Watch TV?' Forgetting himself, Old Conal had raised his voice. He promptly returned to a whisper.

'Quiz shows,' he mouthed, and tapped the side of his nose. 'Quiz shows.'

'What quiz shows? *Come on down*, and all that?' Old Conal nodded. '*Generation Game, University Challenge, Ask the Family, Weakest Link*… all that sort of thing?'

'Aye, and a whole lot more. Every quiz show you can think of.'

'And how did you work out that the government is watching us and monitoring us by watching an oul' simple game show?'

'Did you ever notice…' Old Conal whispered, 'that you never hear the same question asked twice? In the whole history of quiz shows I bet you've never heard the same question asked twice!' All the man from Dromore could do was agree with a slight nod of his head, but all he really wanted was the remedy so he could get crouched in behind a hedge pronto.

'Y' see! It's a set-up! We only hear what they want us to hear!' Now convinced of Old Conal's impending insanity, the man from Dromore, still whispering, asked, 'Any chance of the remedy?'

'The remedy? Ah, the remedy. The Elimination Paradox. I don't have it.'

Stunned, the other muttered, 'You don't have it?'

'No. Anyway it's not something you get, as such. It has to be administered.'

'Can you administer it, then?'

'No no no! Certainly not! That has to be done by Black Susan. Sometimes referred to as the Wise Old Woman of the Waters. She lives on the far coast of Donegal, in the townland of Ballyglass.'

'What!' cried the man from Dromore. 'That's a hunderd miles away!'

'Do you want a full, clear evacuation or not? If you don't, then go home and wait until you explode… it's called internal combustion. If you do, then get on that bike, or hire a taxi, or jump a train, or board a plane. But somehow you must get to Black Susan, the Wise Old Woman of the Waters. Her cottage overlooks the mighty Atlantic… at Ballyglass… beside the rocks. She will show you the Elimination Paradox. Go! Ride like the wind!'

Disheartened and weary and about to detonate, the man from Dromore found his way up through Cavan, past the lakes of Fermanagh in the rain, touched the edge of Tyrone, and found himself of a mild evening in the County of Donegal, some say the most beautiful county in Ireland. But he had no time for sightseeing. He was lost. He asked about, but no-one had ever heard of Black Susan, or the Wise Old Woman of the Waters, or anyone of such peculiar name.

What was the Elimination Paradox? No-one in Donegal had heard of that either. Was it some sort of secret, Masonic-like ritual in which he had to partake; funny handshakes, aprons and goats and things like that? He didn't know if he was up to it or not. All he wanted was a good… but before he could think another thought his mind turned to the broad ocean stretched out before him; millions of living creatures all going to the toilet on a regular basis. He envied them.

His stomach groaned and creaked, sometimes he doubled over with the pain of the cramps, sometimes he bent over and waited, trying to fool his brain into sending the required signal to his bowels. But nothing happened. He was alone and miserable. Like a Beethoven symphony, had he completed his last movement?

He slumped down at the side of a country lane. The grass was dry and the stone wall provided a warm and comfortable rest for his aching back. Oh dear God! he moaned. How had he allowed himself to fall into such a predicament? The wife had been wise to advise an apple a day. She said that bowel problems ran in families: a constipation trait, a 'soft' trait, an irregular trait, an irritable bowel trait. The only way to alleviate a constipation trait was by gorging on good, regular roughage. And as he let his head sink into his arm, he knew he'd failed. He'd failed himself as a man, and he'd failed his wife.

He could hardly keep his eyes open now. He looked down at his boots. Each lace had long since shrivelled to three inches in length, only managing to tie the top two eyes of each boot. He thought of his wee farm at the top of a hill in Dromore. It had been built on the site of an ancient fort, permitting stunning views in all directions. On a clear day he could see the Mournes, sometimes so close he felt he could touch their inky blueness, the Sperrins in the North-West, Slieve

Gullion's braes in the south, and the sheen, like a sword's blade, of Lough Neagh in the vale. He thought of his favourite summer-seat in the yard, from where many a day he had supped his tea and looked out to the shimmering hues of summer on the far hills. He wondered why, sometimes when going to sit on that seat he felt like sitting on the right side of it, and at other times he preferred the left. Life was full of mysteries, but the mystery most on his mind was how he was going to shift this enormous silage pit from his stomach. He smiled faintly when he recalled his home, set up so high it seemed to possess its own weather system. He'd long since given up watching and listening to all forms of weather forecasts on the radio and TV; they simply didn't apply to his farm on the hill. He could look down and tell what the weather was like thirty miles away. It may be summery and fine down there, but on his isolated hilltop it was more than likely cold, cloudy and blustery. It always seemed to be windy. Even on the hottest days of summer there was a breeze, in winter the wind-chill factor was debilitating. Some days at normal altitude there may be a slight breeze blowing, but up on his hilltop a gale of hurricane proportions would be ripping the roofs of his outhouses. He had often joked that at his altitude the washing on the line dried even when it was raining.

He had cursed the man – whoever it was – who had surrounded the house with ash trees, probably as a wind-break. Ash trees of all things. Not only did winter last an extra month at that height, but the ash trees stood lifeless and barren up until damn near the beginning of June, while all the other houses in the glens around where swathed in the lush greenness of sycamores, beeches and oaks. Even so, he wished he were there now, ash trees or no ash trees.

And the yard that was home to three families of starlings, meaning that no matter where he parked the tractor it always seemed to be on the starlings' flight path, and used by them as target practice.

Only last week he'd been driving two of the old cows in for milking when he looked up and caught sight of the first swallows, chittering high up in the sky, then swooping and dog-fighting like they were in the Battle of Britain. His wife had seen them too. She came to the back door wiping her hands on a dish cloth.

'There's the first swallows,' she said cheerily.

'Aye,' said he. 'That's the three-fifteen from South Africa.'

'What are y' doin' lyin' there like a tinker?' she said.

'What are y' talkin' about, wummin?'

'What are y' doin' lyin' agin the wall?'

'The wall? What wall? Who? Where?' he mumbled. He opened his stinging, unfocused eyes to see an old hag bending over him, prodding him with an ash plant.

'I asked y' what you're doin'?' Only two decomposed teeth showed in the dark chasm of her mouth. They reminded him of two fag butts in an ash tray.

'I must've dozed off,' he forwarded.

'Dozed off? Dozed off? You've been fast asleep for a cuppla hours y' lazy bugger y'!'

'I've been walkin' for days,' he said, standing up. 'And I'd take it kindly if you'd quit pokin' me with that stick.' Scratching his head he tried to come to his senses. 'I'm sorry if I disturbed you missus, but I'm lookin' for a woman who may be able to help me. A woman who goes by the name a Black Susan.'

'And what would a tinker like you be wantin' with Black Susan?'

'So you know her then?'

'Might. 'pends who's askin'.'

'She's the only one in the country who knows about the... Elimination Paradox. I need to find her or I'm goin' to...'

'Bust yer boiler?' She laughed out loud, her gaping teeth now grotesque. She laughed and spluttered and nearly choked. 'Oh God, I'm gonna be bad!'

'You know of the problem, then?'

'I can help you,' she managed to say when she'd calmed down. 'Come back to m' house and I'll point y' in the right direction.'

The cottage was a low, thatched cabin, surprisingly immaculately kept, with wild pink roses in a garland over the small front door. The walls and floors were painted emerald green and a huge welcoming turf fire glowed in the grate.

'So it's the Elimination Paradox yer after, is it?'

'Can you help? Please?' The man from Dromore now felt as if he weighed forty stone, and the irresistible soda farls and oat cake which Black Susan served straight off the griddle didn't help his dilemma, but they were delicious.

After a short pause to rake the fire and stack more black turf on the flames the old hag said, 'Well, m' boy. I'm Black Susan, the Wise Old Woman of the Waters or whatever y' want to call me, and in a very short while all yer troubles will be behind you. Hee hee!' He could have kissed her craggy lips in relief!

'What must I do?' he cried, like one needing salvation.

'You must do exactly as I tell you, when I tell you, in every detail. Is that understood? If you don't do as I tell you, you may as well head home right now, although you'll probably combust before you get there.'

'Yes! Anything, anytime, anywhere!'

'Then go and take off every stitch of clothing and stand in the middle of that field that runs down to the shore.' She pointed in the direction of a rutted, rocky field, but the man from Dromore stood stunned.

'What?' he gasped.

'I think you heard me.'

'Every...?'

'Yes. Every.'

The man from Dromore stood naked as a baby in the middle of the field, trying to cover himself as best he could, remembering numerous dreams he'd had throughout his life of finding himself in exactly this predicament. But wakening up now would not relieve him of this embarrassment, as it had done in the past. His white flesh seemed to glow translucently in the evening sunlight. There was no sign of Black Susan, or anybody or anything for that matter for a good twenty minutes during which time he was certain he'd been duped. He considered putting his Long Johns and vest back on and walking home and if, on his homeward journey he exploded in a shower of intestines and silage, well, that's life. Suddenly Black Susan was laughing and shrieking from the gate, about twenty yards away, an evil apparition, howling like a demon whilst trying to bring under control two of the most enormous, most vicious snarling black dogs he'd ever seen. They lunged at the sky, barking, growling, tugging at the ropes which tied them to Black Susan's bony hands. He was staggered that she managed to hold them at all. They yelped and chomped and drooled, at one time almost pulling her right off her feet. The constipated man was frozen with fear – how do you make good your escape over a rocky field in your bare feet? In two seconds' time he was going to find out.

'Go my darlings! Get 'im!' laughed Black Susan, throwing the ropes wildly in the air and letting loose the dogs of Hell. 'The Elimination Paradox!'

'Holy Mother of Jee—!' He turned and ran for his life. He just ran. And ran. As fast as he could in the direction of the Atlantic Ocean. He didn't care if he drowned – he sure as Hell wasn't going to end his life savaged by two curs the size of two small bullocks. He ran faster than he'd done at school sports day, but soon the beasts were gaining on him. He accelerated, but so did they. He could hear their slobbering jaws and thundering feet behind him. They were silent now, but that scared him even more, because he knew there's nothing more devious and dangerous than a silent vicious dog. They lapped at his heels; he could sense their muzzles brushing his ankles. Two Satans on his tail. He was sure that one more surge would see them alongside him and his lower leg would be off in a single bite. He zigzagged wildly, waiting for the final crunch of bone and sinew. In the distance that oul' hoor Black Susan still giggled and shrieked as if it was the funniest thing she'd ever seen in her life, but then again it probably was. He didn't care for his decency any longer; he was unashamedly being beaten to death with his own body parts.

And just as the end was in sight, just as he tensed in wait for the excruciating end to his pathetic life, just as he braced himself for the sensation of fangs through human flesh… a great relief came over him, a sudden and violent evacuation that left him so light and weightless he imagined he could fly. He continued to run, accelerating away from the stinking beasts and plunged himself into the cool blue cleansing waters of Donegal Bay. He was alive! He was safe! He was… empty!

It had worked beyond his wildest dreams. He washed himself and put his clothes back on. The dogs had gone, or had they both been strafed to death? Black Susan had had her entertainment for the day and was probably back home making potato bread and waiting for her fee. The man from Dromore felt better and healthier than he'd ever done in his life as he gaily marched up the laneway to Black Susan's. He needed to thank her from the bottom of his bowel.

But the cottage was gone. Not gone, really, it was but a derelict ruin, with decomposing, rotted thatch and not a sign of a rose over the door. There wasn't even a door. He peeked in through the cobwebbed windows. No sign of the griddle or the black kettle or the turf fire, just damp and stained drab walls and sheep dung. He called out for Black Susan, but his voice died in the empty room.

Attaching his bicycle clips, he headed back to Dromore, whistling a happy refrain.

ANGELA MAGUIRE

I

THERE'S A STRANGE, UNEARTHLY FEELING immediately after a city centre explosion. It's as if the very heart of nature has been violated with something so tremendously unnatural and lethal. Firstly, you become aware of the intense, hollow silence like a vacuum screaming to be filled; a tangible silence that you know is being sensed by every living thing in the vicinity. You instantly imagine an old woman dropping her cup of tea and crying oh heavens what was that? Or the driver feeling the force of the blast on the side of his car. Or the pigeon being suddenly blown off its roost. The whole theatre, for a few long seconds, seems hung in a weird dream state. Then you become thankful that you're still alive and you've missed yet another summons to hell, and you wonder if some person's life ended at the same second as you heard the blast.

I was slightly out of breath from having walked briskly for the quarter mile to the scene of the explosion. I always try to walk and not run to these things when I'm on the beat because it's no use running at full pace and arriving there gasping for air, with people needing your immediate assistance. I'd listened to the radio transmissions, stating that the seat of the explosion was probably in such-and-such a street, then somebody else would come on and say that it sounded as if it was in such-and-such another street. The pall of black smoke usually gave the game away.

Cars were beginning their usual congestion, drivers rubber-necking to see if they could see blood and guts and at the same time bringing the city's traffic to a standstill. Men and women, boys and girls were stepping quickly and rigidly in the opposite direction. I wasn't even near the scene when panicked people stopped me and asked what happened. 'I think it was an explosion,' I offered, sarcastically. It had been a long shift.

As I rounded the corner the sight of blue flashing lights and garish sirens met me. The street was strewn with broken glass, twisted window frames like dead stick insects, and masses of speechless, smouldering rubble, under which was jammed a mangled green car and a mutilated human body slumped at the wheel.

The students of death had struck again, and I cursed them. I didn't know who the man at the wheel was; in this crazy wee country for all I knew it may have been the very terrorist who planted the bomb and scored an own goal, but it was more than likely some poor bugger who happened to be in the wrong place at the wrong time. I was sickened that another life in Ulster's bleak diary of death had been stolen.

The scene of the crime was well sealed off and secured and there was no immediate danger to anyone else, even though the bombed car would have to be checked by army experts in case another, secondary, device was hidden on board. I went across to a young Inspector and waited until his blind panic had subsided a little and asked if there was anything needed doing. He told me to *identify a street* and ensure that no one came close. Dear help him. His heart was in the right place, but at things like this he was more concerned about how he was going to look and sound on the late night news. The same man kept a Bible lying on the back seat of his car for effect. The task he gave me was fair enough; it wouldn't be too taxing and at least I was doing something.

'I take it he's dead,' I said to Big Andy as he ran past me, his face pale and nervous.

'He's tatey bread, all right,' he shouted back at me over his shoulder. 'Defintootely.' His attempts at acting cool and authoritative were an abysmal failure, but at least it was gratifying to know that there were still people in the world who could keep their conversations crisp and to the point. I debated with myself if I wanted to see a mutilated form at that time of the evening, especially when my stomach had been feeling a bit queasy all day. Anyway, on my way across Violet Street I passed the car and peeked in. He lay still and dumb and twisted.

'He's an awful mess,' said Gordon McNamee, a young, green Constable as he walked from the darkness towards me. He had wandered over for a quiet nosey and his first look at a corpse. His words were tense and eerie. His usual youthful exuberance had flown skyward with the frightened pigeons.

'Poor bastard,' I said.

I watched Billy Carson look dejectedly into the wreckage then turn round quickly and viciously punch his open palm. His pupils were dilated and watery and I knew that he had probably been in some working mens' club since the shift began, talking all the drivel of the day just for gratis pints and halfins. But now he was excited about something – unusual for big fat Billy Carson.

'I could've saved him,' he cried, 'but the poor sod went up in flames!'

'Are you all right, Billy?' I asked.

'I feel like shit. I was so bloody helpless. Your worst nightmare.' I knew Billy's form, and I knew it wouldn't be long before some Famous Grouse would be making its way down his neck.

'They reckon it's mistaken identity,' Gordon McNamee said quietly, in his usual self-effacing way, as if he were embarrassed about having more information about the situation than the more senior members, myself included. He hated to appear nosey. Billy Carson was all ears.

'How come?' Billy asked.

'Apparently some plain clothes cop parks his car here most days. They think he let this fella,' (he thumbed into the car) 'have his car for the day while his own was being repaired. But they're not sure.'

'Christ,' Billy said, spitting.

I was amazed at how quickly information and stories appeared from seemingly nowhere. Other people seemed to know where to look and who to ask to get the gen they wanted. I had never perfected that skill. Maybe it was because I just wasn't nosey enough. Maybe I had spent most of my career so far in a state of demotivation… I don't know.

I collected myself and walked across and looked into the car. I saw the tousled hair of the dead man hanging in his dead eyes. Five minutes ago this lifeless thing in a Burton suit was a thinking, breathing, living person. I looked at the short length of leg that someone had hurriedly retrieved and placed back in the car beside him. His black shoe and charcoal grey sock were still on the foot but his calf was ripped and torn like the entrails of a squashed rabbit on the road. I peered at his laces. They were still tied. I thought of him tying those laces this morning beside the breakfast table as he finished his Corn Flakes and toast. He said he would be home late. How right he was.

I returned to my junction and stood for about ten or fifteen minutes. I tied some white tape across the street at waist level, tying it to a drain pipe on one side and a traffic sign on the other – and yet some sharp citizens would come up and stand at the white tape and ask if the street was closed. A sudden whiff of burning flesh in the air made me wretch and I nearly vomited there and then on the footpath. My eye caught the flapping of ruffled feathers between two bin bags. It was a dead pigeon, caught in the blast. The casualties of war.

I soon got fed up listening to the incessant radio transmissions of senior officers arriving at the scene and frantically trying to establish their dominance and authority. It became a power struggle for them, and a grovelling exercise for the toadies. I thought constantly of the poor bugger mutilated at the wheel of another man's car. I mean, how unlucky is that? His wife would probably know by now. I heard the bosses select a very diplomatic Detective Sergeant to do that job. I tried to imagine what state she would be in right this minute. Probably being comforted by a neighbour. The children will have been sent upstairs. The daughter will have been called back from her friend's. From this day forth their lives will never be the same again – just a series of forced adjustments, trying to cope. And the irony is, which seems lost on the faceless fanatics, is that once they slay their victim, they cannot do him any more harm. His life ends in a flash, probably not even feeling pain. The ones who really suffer are the innocent wives who are left as grieving widows and the innocent children bewildered and fatherless and bitter for the rest of their lives. Each so-called political murder trawls in a big family of totally innocent people.

News reporters herded themselves into the street and stood at the tape, cameras click clicking, flashes flashing, beards and suede jackets with fur collars the fashion of the day. Eventually hands were stuck deep into pockets, they began to sway from foot to foot, speaking in deep affected accents, sharing war stories of the scenes of past atrocities. The chrome of their cameras and tripods glinted in the darkness; the beams from their arc lights scanned the sky like the 20th Century Fox logo. When one of the younger, good looking, journalists walked towards me, pulling wisps of long, auburn hair from her face, I greeted her with a confident, professional smile. She smiled a quick pleasant smile and then went serious and asked me if I knew the murdered man's name. No, I didn't. She then went over and began interviewing an elderly man and woman who had both been showered with fragments of glass from a shop window. I think they were both waiting for an ambulance; they were hugging each other, scared, but glad to be alive. He was shaking his head in disgust at the whole outrage. She was sobbing.

The acrid, choking smell of burning plastic, flesh and dust was still with me, clinging to my nostrils, when I heard my name called in one of those familiarly arrogant tones. It was the Chief Inspector – the very man I didn't want to see because I knew he'd put me in an even worse mood – stalking his truculent stalk towards me. He was an ugly, uneducated big man with skin like a dead dog's and a mouth that didn't really open when he spoke. I had always imagined that because of this unnaturally small orifice his breath would be stale and rancid, and yet rumour had it that he was getting it on with the attractive wife of one of his own officers. What women will do to have their brush with power! He was being trailed by Michael Barnes, who was keeping a safe distance. When the boss got to within twenty feet of me he began ranting with his mouth almost closed and throwing his arms about, pointing in twenty directions at once; the sign of a professional idiot.

'Clear those reporters away!' he screamed at me. 'They've no business talkin' to those people!' He kept marching towards me, and I cursed myself for being in the wrong place at the wrong time: in the path of a renegade imbecile. It was not within my ambit to tell him that the reporters were doing their jobs, just like us. He came up to me and said something close up. What he actually said remains a mystery to this day. I became aware of an overwhelming, noxious malodour from his mouth. I gagged at the smoky, ingrained curry stink from his yellow-toothed oral cavity. Really, the man's breath could have dropped a bluebottle in flight at six yards. When the air cleared and I could breathe again, he was gone. Michael Barnes appeared like a genie in front of me, rolling his eyes, and said, 'With assholes like that, is it any wonder we're losin'?'

As Michael walked away tutting he asked if I fancied going for a pint after we'd finished, but by the time the army had made the area safe and the mortuary van had taken the remains away and the damaged buildings were sealed off and boarded up, it would probably be past closing time. I mused at Michael's way. One minute he could be cutting and sarcastic, making you feel clumsy and stupid and the next he would be asking you into his company. He blew hot and cold. Although I wasn't in the mood for drinking, I thought that if we did happen to get somewhere before last orders, I would enjoy the escape from reality at least.

II

VIOLET STREET MARKED THE NORTHERN BORDER of what was the city's pathetic effort at a red light district. In reality it was nothing more than a couple of streets in a commercial enclave where twenty or thirty females loitered, wanton and ugly, each one resembling Myra Hindley, at the street corners and in large office doorways. Some stood dangerously alone, others in groups of three or four. Most were fat and singularly unattractive, smelling of cheap wine and even cheaper perfume. Some had no teeth, one had only one leg, but this didn't seem to deter the punters, who crawled the kerbs with slobbery mouths and lonely eyes.

From where I stood, looking down Violet Street I could see Maggie with new red tights, and when she saw me she gave a curt wave. She was standing in the elaborate back door of a theatre. She wasn't one of the worst looking, there was something plain, yet inviting about her. I'd even found myself on past occasions on the beat, plotting a meandering path so that I could worm my way down Violet Street and chat to her.

I was warmed and cheered when I saw that she had left her post and was walking in my direction.

'You'll do no business tonight with me standin' here,' I said as she walked up and asked for a light.

'I know, love,' she said, 'but I just got dropped off and a need a wee smoke. Do y' not have a light, love?' I told her I didn't – filthy habit – but she stood and yarned in one of the red brick doorways that provided no light. There was a stinking bin liner full of rubbish left at the door. She was friendly and humble, and in the subdued light of the city she didn't look bad at all.

As a law enforcement officer I didn't give a damn about persecuting or prosecuting the city's whores. I always felt there were other, more immediate and important things to be getting on with, like trying to get each side to see the other side's story. I believed that there really would have been more rapes, sexual assaults and child abuse were it not for these women putting their lives on the line for thirty quid a go. What type of girl would get into a car with a total stranger, knowing that the only thing on his mind is sex? But what after that? What goes on inside his mind when he's pulling up his trousers and buckling his belt as he's jammed against his steering wheel? She reaches down to her handbag and offers him a cigarette while lighting one for herself. They're in a darkened secret corner of a car park. Nobody else in sight. If he slits her throat and turfs her onto the hard ground, who will know? Who will care? When I'm talking to the prostitutes sometimes they confide that they are afraid. Worse still, they feel that they are not entitled to the protection of the law because they are carrying out an illegal act in the first place. I tell them that's crap. I insist that they are human beings, making a living as best as they can and that they are entitled to as good a protection as anyone else. Most times my ramblings, however, fall on deaf, usually intoxicated, ears.

Maggie was good crack, with her toothless grin and her bob of bleached hair, and passed about fifteen minutes, chatting about officious policewomen, and rogue policemen with whom she'd been. The bottle of wine was never too far from her lips. I asked her how business was.

'Quiet.' Slug of wine. 'You b's are chasin' the punters away so yar. Y' know love, it's a hundred quid every time I show m' face in court.'

'It couldn't be as bad as that,' I said, smiling. 'Sure a good lookin' woman like yourself would make five times that in a night.'

'Aye right! On yer bike! The likes a me makes nathin' except at the weekends. You're not talkin' to a wee girl y' know. I've been on the street too long, and b's like you don't make my life easy, so y' don't.' I couldn't take offence at her outpouring; she was just that type of person.

'You're one of the better looking ones, I always thought,' I said to cheer her up. She took a long drag on the cigarette jammed between her nail-bitten fingers and sucked in deeply, momentarily closing her eyes.

'I wouldn't say that,' she said, almost shyly.

'Well, who else looks so well in red tights?' She laughed.

'Oh, these? *Stockings*, if you don't mind.' And to prove the point she pulled her skirt up around her waist to expose – with apparent pride – the full gear, in red.

'Very nice,' was all I could manage. I think it must have been the look on my face that caused her to burst out giggling and drop her cigarette. In the second or two that her thighs were uncovered – white and deliciously fleshy – I tried manfully to take in as much of this unusual spectacle as possible but was panicked at the fear of one of the bosses poking his big red Masonic nose round the corner.

Maggie turned serious. 'Look at wee Angela. She's a wee cracker. Only twenty, y' know. Two kids. Diff'rent da's.'

'Okay,' I had to agree, 'she is a beauty, but there's not many more like her.'

'Speak a the divil...' said Maggie as she hitched her skirt back down. I was still musing on the lusts of the flesh when I followed Maggie's eyes along to the end of the street. 'Here she is.'

I looked back down the street to where a small chapel was illuminated tastefully with spotlights to see the slim and beautiful figure of Angela Maguire stepping towards us, almost hesitatingly. Her long, toned legs tapering perfectly to her ankles and micro-mini skirt were in silhouette, but the walk was unmistakable.

Angela had been doing business for about a year, and in that time we'd enjoyed some great crack about punters, police and the price of a poke. On exceptionally cold nights when I was on mobile patrol in one of the pathetically undisguised armoured vehicles, I would invite her in for a minute to warm herself and chew the fat.

'Hiya,' she said.

'Did y' get any drink, love?' Maggie asked her before I could open my mouth.

'Wise up Mags. I'd to buy the wee fella a new buggy today. I'm stony broke.' I felt sorry for her. When she turned to me with a wry smile I said Hiya Angela. I think she was a bit taken aback that I knew her name, but it was easy to remember because it suited her.

'Is somebody dead?' she asked in her drawled Belfast accent.

'Yea,' I said, 'a bomb under a man's car – well, it wasn't actually his car. We don't know who he is yet.'

'That's terrible,' said Angela as she lit a cigarette from the glowing tip of Maggie's, and I could see tears forming in the corners of her eyes. 'Somebody's son. Somebody's da. Somebody's husband. What a waste,' she added.

Under the same crimson light of Violet Street that made Maggie appear above average in looks, Angela was made to appear almost angelic. She had the figure of a model and her hair was blond and cut in a sort of fifties style. She wore her negligible mini skirt and matching jacket with a black lacy thing underneath. When she smiled, her whole body seemed to smile. When I told her she was looking great tonight she blushed and said she was too skinny. I thought she looked perfect.

Maggie could talk under water. She went on and on and on and all I could do was steal an occasional smile from Angela while trying like hell to keep some sort of conversation going. Maggie eventually let up from her ravings about lack of money and police harassment and asked what I was doing after work. I was momentarily stunned and couldn't think of a reasonable answer. I knew what she was hinting at, so I told her I would just be heading home.

'Y' don't fancy a wee bitta bizz later on, do y'?' she said eventually, smiling, so that she had an escape route if I took it thick. Angela looked away shyly. She'd probably never, in her short career, witnessed a cop being propositioned by a prostitute. To her that sort of thing wouldn't be on, but I supposed she'd learn in time. There's no way I would have done business with Maggie, but I didn't want to give her a sharp rejection just in case she held a party or something some time and would invite me, and bring Angela along in the current. I imagined what it would be like to peer at those glossy legs for an entire evening, chatting and laughing and getting to know Angela better. So I put Maggie off by telling her you never know your luck.

Angela smiled and looked up at the night sky, way above the street lights and slate roofs and red brick chimneys.

'Well, I'll be standin' here no doubt when you finish your work, love,' Maggie added. I saw the phallic end of a bottle of cheap wine rousing in her leather-look handbag, and I couldn't believe my luck when she shrugged and said she'd better be heading on to get a bit of business done because she had a fridge to pay off. 'Maybe seeya 'bout twelve, then,' she said as she staggered unsteadily off, hitching up her red stockings as a last persuasion. I panicked because I knew that any chat with Angela would only last a few minutes before I had to go. Michael Barnes was removing the white tape from the lamp posts at the other end of the street. I wanted to talk to her so badly.

'It's not often you're over at this end,' I said politely, turning my attention and body fully towards her, blocking out the outside world.

'I'm not. Just heard the explosion. That's a disgrace, y' know. Poor man. I suppose he has a wife and kids and now they're left without a daddy. I don't know how people can do that sort a thing.' I made some non-committal remark about the country being in such a bad state. She seemed to not really be interested in what I said, but happy enough to stand for a while, sometimes leaning into my personal zone, as close as a pickpocket, and then retreating. She had that annoying habit of cutting into the last words of your sentence, just as you're about to deliver the punch line, with something unrelated, spoiling the effect of what you were going to say. But I forgave her foible.

I heard on the pocket phone that the army bomb disposal team had just about finished and I knew the area would be clear in about fifteen minutes. Then in half an hour the car and body would be removed. Within the hour standby crews of joiners, plumbers and glaziers would be out on double time to repair the damage. It had become one perfectly practised routine. Traffic would flow down the street again, unknowing, and life would continue on as normal. By tomorrow morning there would be no trace of the incident which took an innocent man's life. It reminded me of the movie Westworld, where repair men emerged in the middle of the night and dragged away the injured and malfunctioning robots. I hoped that Angela would stay to the last minute.

She had a beautiful way of looking at you if you said something complimentary about her. I sneaked in a couple of wee observations like her hair was nicely styled or that she's lost weight but suited it, things like that. And each time she looked shyly away and the corners of her lips turned up in a cute smile with dimples and I could have very easily reached out and taken her cold hand. We chewed the fat for about ten minutes, talking about everything and anything and yet nothing, but my mind was going crazy to find out why she was standing with me when there was good tax-free money to be made on the streets round the corner. She didn't give me any real indication, but I couldn't stop myself from harbouring the possibility that she fancied me; I mean *really* fancied me, and not just my hard-earned cash. I was getting these tremendous vibes and yet she'd hardly once looked me straight in the eyes. I kept telling myself to catch myself on, but the attraction wouldn't go away.

She stood in the doorway of a dark empty building that had a polished brass name plaque on one side. I moved slightly closer to her so that if you looked down the street from where the ATO was you wouldn't have suspected there was anybody in the street at all. We were talking in whispers and there didn't seem to be another sound in the whole city. I wasn't listening for anything anyhow. I wanted more than anything to kiss those lips. What was I thinking? I had no drink in me to break down barriers of inhibition. I found myself thinking *go on, step out into the unknown*. Then a jolt of realisation hit me. If I kissed her she could take off up the street to my favourite Chief Inspector and allege rape, or sexual assault or something. That's *all* I would need.

The intermittent conversation must have lulled for a minute while my head pounded with possibilities. She said she thought she'd better be going. I had to act now. I stepped an inch forward so that I was face to face with her and I bent down and kissed her. It wasn't just a peck on the cheek. She turned her full lips towards me and you'd think we had been lovers for five years. She clung round my neck, tossing what hair I had and edging that sensuous body ever closer to mine. I cursed the uniform that I had on; there must have been about three layers including body armour, gun, belt, holster pocket phone and field dressings, but my imagination ran berserk when I realised what was happening.

The radio continued to blare out its static-hissed messages minutes later when I came up for air, gasping and drunk with desire. I could taste her wine and smoky saliva in my mouth. I felt that this person had just isolated her working life from her private. She stared silently at me. I smiled. She smiled back. A confident smile.

We kissed warmly and deeply again. I was becoming a man; I felt the young contours of her back under her jacket, the touch of soft cotton, and her buttocks were hardly covered as I kneaded them like dough. A small writhing body. Two people locked in a strange embrace in a back street while a man lay dead in a car with his head severed, and I collected all my courage and arranged to see her later that night when I finished work.

Angela walked away, her sleek curves stepping awkwardly proud in high heels and her handbag carried by the strap so that the bag nearly touched the flagstones with each step. She looked over her shoulder and smiled. Was I the biggest eejit that ever lived, or what? She was after my money, that was all. I was flattering myself to even think she liked me, but men are gullible. I was gullible. I sneered at the argument that as far as the sex trade is concerned, women are being exploited. I thought of the men at night clubs with their tongues drooling over a lap dancer and paying twenty quid for a pint of beer, of expensive hotel rooms and massage parlours with high-priced extras and coy ladies getting rich and I wondered who it really is that's getting exploited.

The air turned cold and my breath hung like a ghost in front of me. All I wanted to do now was get away from work. I would have murdered for a hot whiskey, but decided a cup of tea before I left would do. The moon hung like a silver plate amid occasional stars and skittering cotton wool clouds.

My mind wandered. I felt uneasily happy. A bittersweet anxiety. The Sergeant was waving at me with exaggerated gestures of his whole arm. He reminded me of a windmill. There were a couple of plain clothes men about – detectives and forensic officers – and I reckoned that, as usual with messy scenes, I would be handed a dirty yard brush and told to sweep up the debris, grumbling that brushing the streets was never part of the job description.

'Givvus a hand out with him, lad,' said the CID Inspector straight to my face, and then nodded towards the crumpled car. My stomach churned to a halt. The delights of Angela Maguire and our clandestine rendezvous disappeared in an instant.

I walked over slowly, hoping that someone else would suddenly appear and do the job for me. Nobody appeared. I didn't want to do this job; there's something so eerie and unnatural about a lump of dead flesh that used to be a human being. If you stare long enough you'll see a dead person breathe.

They laid out a plastic sheet on the ground near what was left of the driver's door. They had organised arc lights, glaringly aimed at the wreckage, exaggerating shapes and colours.

'Try to get him out all in one piece,' somebody said behind me. Somebody else climbed in through the passenger's door to push. The Detective Inspector took the dead man's collar and pulled him back onto the seat. The dead man's eyes were half open. His face was still recognisable as that of a human being, but that was about all.

'Okay,' said the Detective Inspector, 'after three.' I reluctantly took hold of the man's arm. He wore a dark blue pin-stripe suit. I touched the material, trying not to feel the body underneath, but I had to take a better grip so I grabbed his whole forearm. I could feel the shape of dead muscle underneath the clothing. I gave a quick glance around me. Everyone else seemed okay. Somebody reached forward and straightened the dead man's head so that it didn't hang to one side. Me, I just wanted to be anywhere else in the world. This wasn't my job. They could stuff it. We heaved and pulled and pushed and he came away in two pieces. His trunk was hauled onto the street but his lower abdomen and legs remained in the car, under a stew of entrails.

'Thanks lad,' said the Detective Inspector later. 'Bit of a mess, eh?'

'Is that us finished?' I asked the Sergeant when I got back to the station.

'Yea… straggle on. You orright?'

'Yea…'

'Mixed up crazy world… See y' tomorra.'

'Night.'

I had a shower and sat at the end of a single bed in the dormitory on the top floor of the station. For some reason, maybe because of all the things that happen in this muddled up wee island, my mind went back to our farm in the country, and my father, and the couple of hundred acres he cared for as if the soil had been given him as a precious gift from God. It was a paradise that gave me, as a child, unlimited freedom to play either in the flat meadows or the tree-covered glen, where a small stream laughed and roped its way under sycamores and oaks. My father planted two seedlings every time he cut a tree down, and planted two hedges for every hedge uprooted. He loved that land. Even the smell of it. I never remember seeing barbed wire until I ventured further out into the world, when I was shocked to find that other farmers' boundaries were marked with wire, concrete posts, brick walls, corrugated tin, wooden pallets, car bonnets; all the unsightly items they could muster. Instead, to mend a fence I watched Dad heading out with nothing but a saw and a pair of heavy gloves. He would saw through a thick branch or bough to about half way. Then he would twist it downwards and across until it filled the gap. He would weave it into place – mostly it would be a thorn hedge or blackthorn so that was when he needed the gloves. So the end result was a neat, rustic, living hedge, like a long finger of woven branches; an enduring piece of workmanship. When we used to moan and groan about having to walk a hundred yards to the bus stop in the mornings he used to jokingly boast that when he was my age he was able to use a horse plough, and a man had to walk eleven miles to plough one acre.

Although his death certificate proclaimed *heart attack*, I knew after a while, on reflection, that the heart business was only half the story. It was the country in which he lived that caused his death. For sixty years he had tended that land; his land. His fields were the pride of the countryside. But one nippy day in March as he walked along, checking the hedges and looking forward to the intense activity that spring heralded, about four soldiers with heavy camouflage jumped out on him from a thicket. The initial shock gave him a start and he became scared as the four black-faced squaddies trained their rifles on him and shouted orders in their English accents. And their line of questioning annoyed him.

'What's your name?' one asked viciously, but before my dad could answer, another piped up,

'What are you doing here?'

'I'm just checkin' on m' sheep… there they are… over there…'

'Where do you live?'

'In that house there… in the holla…' One soldier got his notebook out and started writing. My dad said with a tremble in his voice, 'There's never any trouble around here… why were y' hidin'?'

'*We* ask the questions, Paddy. You just keep quiet.'

After further interrogation on that spring day, my dad returned home a ruined man.

'What has become of this country that an honest man can't walk his own land without being examined by some young English upstart?' It was his type, his sensitivity that made him go downhill from there. The country was changing for the worse, and he felt too old and too stolid to change with it. And when helicopters began flying over his fields at a hundred feet, causing ewes to prematurely drop their embryonic lambs in fear, and calves to flounder in ditches when the mothers fled in panic, my father just gave up the will to live.

III

MEMORIES OF MY FATHER HAD DEPRESSED ME and stuck to me like an uninvited visitor. I looked Michael Barnes up and told him I didn't fancy going for a beer. He said he would see me tomorrow. I phoned my wife and told her I'd be late… because of the bomb and all.

I got into my car and sat dumb for a minute until the muddiness left my head. I looked at my watch. I would meet her in half an hour. I drove to the nearest off-licence and bought a few cans of beer and a small bottle of vodka. Then I drove to the arranged rendezvous and waited. The dying engine was my death knell, telling me I had finally done it. An angel on one shoulder was telling me to start the engine and go home, but the other, on the other shoulder was louder and more persuavive, and in some ways more tuned in and appropriate to how I was feeling.

I waited until ten past and wondered if I should call it a night. A car pulled in in front of me. My head thudded. The backs of two heads. One male, one female. It was Angela. With a man. God, this could be a set-up and my police warrant card photograph will be on the front page of the News Letter in the morning. I sat my ground, breathing heavily. The thought of her having had sex with that man – if he wasn't a terrorist – within the last ten minutes turned my stomach. But I had no reason to complain. Was I not as dirty an old man as the nameless head in front?

'Hiya,' she said as her long bare legs stepped into the car. She looked at me, held her glance for a second and smiled.

'Hi,' I said, and coughed; just to make a sound. I smelt her perfume. Roses. Cheap roses. The man in front drove off, his diesel Merc rumbling with a loose exhaust. I tried to put the things that he had been doing with her out of my head. It was hard.

'You're lookin' great,' I said.

'Am I late?'

'Nope,' I said quickly, and then, 'Where do you usually go?' She didn't answer, so I kept driving out of the city.

'I don't care where we go…' she said, snuggling into the seat.

'Any ideas? Would you like to go for a drink first… or something?'

'Well…' Before she could answer I asked her if she'd been busy since I saw her last.

'Not really.'

'I hope you made enough to see you over Christmas.'

'No, I didn't. I didn't stay about too long after I was talkin' to you.'

'Why not?' Again she was slow to answer.

'What about gettin' something from the offy and going to my flat?' she said. I was able to produce the vodka and beer from the back seat as if by magic.

'Do y' keep those for emergencies?' she laughed. I tucked the bottle into the glove compartment so it didn't roll about and left the cans, like six little silver soldiers, on the back seat. She was combing her hair with long sensuous sweeps to the side. I kissed her cheek. She let her hand stray to the back of my neck. She was twiddling with my hair as we sat for a moment, just looking at one another and smiling. Then I felt uncomfortable and started the engine.

Directing me to her flat, she explained it was a different place from where she lived with her kids. She shared the dingy apartment with another girl, not mentioning if she was a prostitute as well; maybe just expecting me to assume. Along the way we had a laugh at a couple of things she told me about the other girls who worked the streets. It was her life, and suddenly I felt sorry for her. She was a quiet, vulnerable girl in a big, trashy world. I reached over and took her hand and she grasped mine as if her life depended on it and caressed my thumb. I could feel those old familiar tingles shoot to every bodily extremity. She sidled across to me and I touched her legs for the first time. It was like touching cold silk. She put her arm round me as I was still driving, and still trying to find my way among the maze of red-bricked terraces. When I pulled up on the kerb she kissed me quickly on the cheek and got out.

'Come on in,' she said, coyly.

The flat was dark when we got in, but a fire was glowing red and orange in the grate. The place smelt like a charity shop and was simply decorated with the usual unmatching ornaments and colours, an old record player beside a portable TV and a bed in the corner with a blue continental quilt.

'When did you light the fire?' I asked.

'Just before I went down to meet you,' she said, taking off her jacket and exposing ivory skin arms, one displaying a blotchy tattoo. She unscrewed the top of the vodka with practised dexterity. I hissed open a can of beer. Then I looked at the made bed and tried to imagine her and her previous client – the one in the diesel Merc – performing right there; him grunting through his hairy nose, dandruff falling from his eyebrows, telling her what he liked and making her do it, rolls of yellow dead-pig fat and a hairy belly rolling over her.

She didn't seem to be in too much of a hurry to get on with business, especially when she went and got two glasses, even though I was contentedly sipping beer from the can. She handed me one to pour her vodka, added some pure orange and then glided across the room and lay on the bed, in that darkened corner. She wasn't making any effort to be seductive; she just was. I stood at the side of the bed, looking down at her, took a stiff swig and sat down at her feet. I slid round and brought my feet up so that we were lying side by side.

'I've something to tell you,' she whispered. I raised my eyebrows in question; I was ready for anything. 'I've fancied you for a long time. I couldn't believe it when you wanted to see me.' I fell instantly in love with this woman whose honesty left me breathless. I must have looked surprised.

'I didn't know that's how you felt. God… if I would've known that!'

'Did you not know I was dyin' for you to ask me out?'

'Y' know,' I said, 'cops and prostitutes are supposed to be on opposite sides of the law, aren't they?' And I immediately regretted calling her a prostitute to her face. To me she wasn't one anymore. 'Well,' I said, returning to the murky business of payment. 'Is it thirty?' She put her hand over mine as I fumbled in my pocket.

'This one's free,' she said. I held her hand, knowing that I would leave her some cash; if not for her at least she could spend it on the kids. I ran my hand over her soft naked hip and down her leg.

'I always saw you around and always admired you, but I never thought it would come to this,' I said.

'I'm glad it has. Are you?' she said, and turned her quivering body towards me.

'You're my first tonight,' she whispered later, which stopped me stroking and kissing her shoulders in surprise. I sat up.

'What about the others…? The guy in the car…?

'When I knew I was seein' you I just came up and got the fire lit and the heat on so that we could have a real cosy wee night together.'

'What about the fella who left you off down the street?'

'That was a taxi, stupid! I thought you cops would know all the number plates!'

'I'm good, but I'm not *that* good!' I said, and she pretended to slap me on the shoulder for my foolishness. I said nothing, but ran my hand from her shoulder to each supple breast, tracing little circles on her skin.

I sat up on my knees and looked down at her.

'You are beautiful,' I whispered, and ran my hands up the flanks of her bare legs.

'Look at my legs!' she laughed. 'They're lily white!'

'I don't care if they're Lily Savage!' I said, and pounced. We made love – no, we didn't make love, (that sounds too romantic), we *had sex* – so violently and animalistically that at one stage I thought the retinas had detached from my eyeballs.

As the fire grew weaker, we were lying in almost total darkness, skin to skin. I combed my hand through her hair as she snuggled close to me, whimpering like a puppy. She dozed the odd time and I allowed myself to do the same, even though the pillow felt as if it was stuffed with hard-backed novels.

Angela sat up and took another drink. She looked drowsy, but her smile was still electrifying. I lay on my back, still caressing different parts of her body in rotation. About fifteen minutes later, when my pulse had slowed enough to get a breath, I asked if I could see her again. She was lying as relaxed as a baby in my arms.

'Anytime,' she said happily. 'I'll give you my number before you go.'

When I came round again the room had grown cold, but heat, and the aroma of womanhood was still oozing from her sleeping body. I slipped my hand over the back of her shoulders, down her sinuous spine and touched the backs of her legs without waking her. I got out of bed, naked and exposed, and put some more coal on the fire. She didn't waken. I put my clothes on, gave her a kiss on the forehead, and let myself out.

WHERE THE SOUL GOES

THOMAS WALSH'S OLD HORSE, NELSON, was his usual self that morning at feeding time, but by afternoon Thomas's wife Sandra rang him at work and said that Nel was lying down in the loose box and wouldn't get up. He had been writhing about, flailing with his hooves, and was in obvious pain. Sandra sounded worried. It was so unlike the old healthy animal, and not being a vet, all Sandra could say was that he was off colour and not himself. 'Phone the vet,' said Thomas, 'and I'll see the boss about getting home as soon as I can.'

By the time he got home – having broken all speed limits to do so – he was surprised to see Nelson up and seemingly enjoying a bucket of feed and a couple of chopped apples. He was back to his usual old self. 'That's strange,' said Sandra almost apologetically. 'Soon after I rang you I went to check on him and there he was – up and about and wanting to get out to the paddock! I didn't bother phoning the vet.'

'All's well in the world then,' said Thomas, relieved. 'And now that I'm home I wouldn't mind a mouthful of tea.' But no sooner were the words out of his mouth when the horse became agitated and unsettled, and soon was struggling to lower himself onto his front knees so that he could lie down again.

'Right, we'll definitely call the vet this time,' said Sandra.

The vet was a ruddy faced man with an Ulster-English accent and a neck that could've been the neck of a rugby player. Long, painful minutes passed in silence as he prodded and felt and pulled. Thomas and Sandra exchanged hopeful, then hopeless glances as the vet mmmed to himself. 'You've a very sick animal here, Mister Walsh,' he said, still checking the insides of Nelson's eyelids. They were dull and bloodless. The long plastic glove was produced and after a thorough internal examination the vet looked disheartened. 'Not good,' he tutted, 'not good. The gut's twisted… peritonitis.' Even though Thomas knew from long association with all things equine that the word peritonitis strikes a dismal chord in the heart of any horse owner he still felt obliged for Nelson's sake to ask was there anything, anything at all could be done. 'The poison's right through his system y' see; that's where the damage is done,' the vet advised. 'Like a badly burst appendix in us humans…'

Thomas and Sandra looked at their pet lying on the grass in obvious discomfort. Thomas shook his head. 'You just don't know what a day will bring, do y'?' Then slowly Nel raised himself up yet again, struggling to his feet. Was there hope yet? Nel began munching on the grass at the edge of the yard. Again he seemed happy enough, but the vet shook his head.

'It's only a brief respite,' he said. 'With each spasm the pain will get worse.' He returned some equipment to the back of his little white van, saying something like that's the way it goes. Pity.

The unpromising look returned to Thomas's face. Sandra was just about managing to hold back tears as Nel, enjoying his lapses from pain, continued to chomp on the grass, lifting his head occasionally to look around and probably wonder what all the fuss was about. 'He's been a member of this family for…' Thomas began to say to the vet, but the quiver in his voice let him down.

'I know, I know,' said the vet objectively, 'but these things happen.' After a pause, like the pause after a minister's final prayer over the dying, he said, 'It's only a matter of time. You don't want him to die in pain. I'll have to do the needful.' Thomas's stomach sank to his feet. Sandra turned away, pale.

'Well, if it has to be it has to be,' said Thomas. 'How do you do it?' he added, with no enthusiasm.

'If you have a gun I could use that...' Thomas shook his head. He didn't have a gun; he'd never had the need for one.

'Injection, then,' the vet said. Thomas nodded. That seemed more humane, and, almost comically, less painful. 'It's really just an overdose of anaesthetic,' the vet advised. The thought sickened Thomas to his heart, but he didn't – couldn't – watch his old friend suffer any more. 'I'll take a dander down the road for a minute,' the vet said with consideration, '...give youse a bit of time.'

When the vet was out of earshot all Thomas could muster was a long, exasperated, 'Christ.' It summed up his shock, sadness, and frustration as he looked up at the tall beeches that surrounded the yard, about to burst forth with the coming spring. 'Poor old fella,' said Sandra, stroking his forehead, between his ears. He loved to be scratched between his ears. She pulled affectionately at his long mane, running her hand over the Prophet's Thumb indentation on his neck.

'Where will we bury him?' Thomas asked, the words choking in his throat. Sandra looked suddenly at the horse, hoping he hadn't heard those fatal words.

'It doesn't seem right to be talking about burying him while he's still here... alive.' It was silly, but no-one laughed, or was even amused.

Thomas remembered how they had more or less saved Nel from a disinterested, vicious farmer, whom they believed had a penchant for hitting him with a bucket, and probably anything else which came to hand. For months no-one could get near the new horse with a bucket, empty or not. The look of fear that came over the animal's eyes – the whites showing in fright – made Thomas and Sandra wonder with sadness what those terrified eyes had witnessed in their day. But with patience and kindness and understanding soon the bucket became something associated with pleasant food; not anything to be feared.

And even when, at the time of the purchase, the farmer had to give Thomas three hundred pounds change from a thousand-pound note, the farmer had secretly rolled the notes together and given the bundle to Sandra. When it was counted later it was found to be a hundred pounds short; typical of the man's ethos in life. But at least they had a wonderful horse. For years Thomas and Nel were inseparable; they trekked everywhere, learned to round up cows and sheep, their children learned to ride safely on his trusty back. Once, when a Friesian bull became separated from his harem by reason of a gate swinging closed in his face, the bull turned to face Thomas and Nel, in its bovine mind accusing them of causing the separation. Thomas's first reaction was to get off the horse and make a run for it; the bull was only thirty feet away but his thinking was that horse and man could split up and confuse the snorting beast. But he remembered from his Western novels and movies that a good horseman stays on the horse's back and braves the attack together no matter what. The bull lowered his head and bellowed a deep, threatening growl. It was a terrifying noise. Thomas felt that an attack was imminent, but then an amazing thing happened. Thomas saw Nel's ears point forward and then back, flattening themselves at the side of his head. Nel looked mean, savage almost. The bull squared up now and pawed the ground. Thomas felt not one single flinch in the little horse below him as Nel lowered his head, mimicking the bull, and with his eyes fixed on the ring through the bull's snout uttered an unearthly, satanic growl that even scared the rider. Low and menacing. Where did that come from? Thomas felt himself ask. The bull seemed to cower at this; it flinched and moved reluctantly away, still eyeballing Nel and his bewildered rider. It slunk away from the gate, so far that Thomas was able to gently walk Nel over and lean down and open the latch. The bull, in gratitude trotted away off to his herd.

Thomas and Sandra spoke at length, quietly under the canopy of the stables, saddened that old Nel's days were over. The vet, having finished his walk, was ready. 'This is it,' said Thomas, and Sandra walked off into the house to mind the children. Anyway, it was all too hard to bear. She glanced over her shoulder for one last look at Nel.

Thomas stroked the horse's forehead and ears. They were warm and soft and full of life. He patted the forelock to make it neat. The vet checked the syringe at the back of the van.

'Wherever you are going,' Thomas whispered into Nel's ear, making sure the vet couldn't hear him, 'whatever happens to you in the next couple of minutes remember one thing; we will never forget you, big man. We all loved and enjoyed every minute you were with us, and you were the loveliest...' The vet approached with deliberation and Thomas's words faded away. He patted the horse's neck and mane; he just wanted to touch him and let him know... The vet held the syringe high, checking its lethal contents against the sky. Thomas patted Nel's neck again and cupped his muzzle and said, 'Good luck, big fella... thanks for everything.'

The syringe barely seemed to touch the animal's neck until the horse's legs gave way and he toppled – half a ton of horseflesh – to the ground at Thomas's feet. There was no sound. Maybe there was, but Thomas didn't hear it. The horse's legs now quivered and his eyes half closed; glazed and dull. Thomas crouched and patted the animal's forehead and muzzle. Breathing was laboured, both for horse and man. The vet stood, a big healthy man in Wellington boots with hands on his hips and a stethoscope dangling from his neck.

'That might not do it,' he said, shaking his head, and went back to the van to get another lethal injection.

'Be brave, Nel,' Thomas whispered. 'We'll miss you.'

As the horse lay – a great mound in the middle of the stable yard – the vet administered another dose. Some blood now trickled down Nel's neck. Thomas cupped the eye that faced upward in his hand;

trying to get him to close it and therefore summon a peaceful, twilight death. The vet sounded the animal's chest.

'You know what I'm going to tell y'? That wee horse doesn't want to die; he's holding on to life for all he's worth. Must've had a good life…' Thomas's own heart churned in his chest. He felt he was going to be sick with grief, but he kept stroking the animal, knowing that death – even if the vet was forced to administer another twenty injections – would eventually come.

The family's border collie, a faithful, lovable pet called Gypsy, sauntered across the yard, meandering shyly over to Thomas. Much to Thomas's surprise, Gypsy – as if feeling the sorrow – sat down beside him and looked down at the giant life form on the ground. It must have seemed strange to the dog, Thomas thought, to be now looking down on something that she had spent her life looking up at. She leaned over a couple of times and licked the horse's face. Then she nuzzled into Thomas, unbidden; then nuzzled strangely close to Thomas's side, nudging, looking him straight in the eye sometimes with her kind, chocolate eyes. She licked his face. At one time the dog almost made Thomas lose his balance.

Then the two cats – kept on the small farm mainly for keeping the mice and rat population at bay – stretching and yawning, strayed into the yard. Both sat under the canopy of the loosebox, staring… staring. In fact Thomas had never seen them stare so much, or look so wide-eyed. They sat side by side as if in need of support, bolt upright with their ears pointed and those two sets of eyes staring. Just staring at something.

'Never in my puff,' the vet tried to joke. 'One more should do it.' The horse's giant chest heaved and groaned. Breathing became almost unnoticeable, except for an occasional puff through his nostrils. Thomas, waiting for the fateful moment when the great chest would heave no more, glanced over at the cats, still bolt upright, still almost hugging one another, still their eyes wide and gaping. Gypsy became agitated, pawing, licking Thomas's face, then intently watched the air above the dying horse like a nun at devotion. Thomas stroked the horse, comforted him. Gypsy pushed fearfully against him while the two cats watched, now with a look of abject terror.

Something was happening.

Suddenly, Thomas was looking down at himself. He was looking down at himself from above the hayshed, even higher than the four beech trees with buds ready to open. He was moving slowly in the sky, floating above the weather-vane with its lady holding her umbrella against the wind. He saw the shape of the horse sprawled on the ground, like one killed suddenly in battle, its legs unnaturally gangly and useless. He saw himself, silently caressing the dying beast, head bowed. He saw the dog cowering uncomfortably beside him. Under the canopy of the loosebox, the cats stared. He floated above this theatre and then the vet said, 'I think that's him…' and Thomas would later remember what happened next as a turbulence, an invisible battle in the air, a sucking feeling… and Nel was gone.

He stroked the lifeless body until Sandra came out and began to cry. Gypsy gave Nel's muzzle one last lick and sauntered off back to her world of dog things. The cats were playing tag with one another in the dust of the yard as if nothing had happened.

Within an hour the farmer next door had excavated a hole under the beech trees with his digger and buried Nel. No-one was sure of the legality of such an action, but Thomas was adamant that there should be no abattoir for his old horse.

Always a great believer in the idea of hard work helping to overcome grief, after a few quiet tears in his bedroom, Thomas braced himself and with a shovel and a wheelbarrow sat about cleaning out the stable. The shape of Nel's body remained embedded in the wood chips, but he pressed on and soon the horsey smell in the air was just a memory.

Evening had descended by the time he had finished, the sky a pale grey with rain clouds thick on the horizon. As he had worked his mind had tried to trace Nel's life, wondering where Nel had been born, in what field had he pranced about as a foal, what his mother was like, had he any brothers or sisters? These were things Thomas had felt no urge to find out while his horse was alive, but now that he was gone he wanted to cling on to every available memory, and even find out more. He switched the porch light on... but nothing. The bulb had blown. Typical, he thought to himself as Sandra walked across the yard towards the car. Her eyes were still red and watery.

'I need some things at the shops. Do you need anything?' she asked.

'Nah,' said Thomas miserably. But the car wouldn't start. The engine tried to turn over but the battery was flat. Double typical.

'Sure it's late, I'll get her jump-started in the morning.'

'What time is it?' asked his wife. Thomas looked at his watch. 3.30pm. 3.30? It was later than that, for sure. His watch had stopped at the time of Nel's departure.

Feeling drained, with that empty-shell feeling of having lost a friend, both Thomas and Sandra sat down to supper. The kids were in bed, unaware as yet of life's hard twists and turns and the feeling of loss.

'...and to add insult to injury,' said Sandra, rolling her eyes, 'a ring on the cooker isn't working.' In danger of disappointment overload, Thomas went to bed.

But as he lay, restless and sleepless and knowing he was in for a night of weird dreams – one which would surely be the revelation that Nel hadn't really died at all and that he was alive and well out in the loosebox and the story of his death had just been one big misunderstanding – he remembered the cats' staring eyes, Gypsy nudging him, the vet saying that the horse didn't want to give in, the aerial view he'd had of the scene, and the brute, twisting, feral, uncontrolled sucking sensation as Nel eventually succumbed, and he wondered, with a terrible fear, what it was that the cats and the dog had actually seen. Outside the planes of human sight and understanding – a sixth sense long since lost in man's scientific, pragmatic existence – had these animals watched some sort of drama unfold before them, a battle invisible to the human eye between life and death enacted above the dying horse? The horse, ferociously wanting to cling to life, feeling by instinct alone that its time shouldn't be up yet, but nature, God, energy – whatever you want to call it – decreeing that no, this animal's time is up and its soul, spirit – whatever – must once again return to the reservoir of souls... but not without a fight as far as Nel was concerned. He thought of the many times when he'd heard of clocks stopping in the rooms of the dead. Whatever powerful event the animals had witnessed that afternoon, it would be easy to believe that one single breath of that energy would be sufficient to halt a pendulum or draw the power from a timid battery. And what about the failure of the electrical appliances? The porch light, the car battery, his watch, the ring of the cooker? The energy seemed, as a by-product of the battle, to have been sucked from these as well, like the innocent dying in a war.

Thomas now shuddered as his mind asked wild and unanswerable questions. Was all life on Earth simply *electricity*, drawing from the electromagnetic field round the planet, driving and powering every living thing? And when the physical body of an animal fails, is the power, the electricity, sucked out of it and returned to the main current, awaiting the conception of a new life? And where does God figure in all this? Did early man sense this unfathomable power around him, encompassing everything, giving life and taking life away, naming it God but not knowing that future man would call it *electricity*?

But Nel was gone. That was enough to think about. Whatever it was that called him back had won the battle, and his empty shell now lay at peace under the beech trees in the garden. Mentally and emotionally drained, Thomas slipped towards uneasy sleep, beckoning happy memories of being on Nel's broad back, grooming his long mane and tail until they shone, the warm, sweet smell of his neck, the clip of his hooves on the stable yard, his kind eyes. An overwhelming sadness at the loss of a friend.

THE ARTIST

THE ARTIST HATED INTERRUPTIONS. If someone knocked at the door while she was working, or called uninvited, or the phone rang – anything designed to deviously seize her attention – her concentration was lost, the moment had flown, maybe until the next day. She compared this need for absolute focus to swimming in the sea; as she squeezed out the paint, selected her brushes, poured her turpentine into paint-splattered jam jars, prepared herself mentally for the battle which was due to commence on the canvas propped on her easel, this was like floating on the surface, treading water, preparing to dive and become ensconced in a fluid, unearthly world. Once ready, she dabbed the brush into the paint and the paint onto the white canvas, almost fearfully; a first stroke as important as a baby's first step into the unknown. The beginning of something, the end result of which she only has a vague notion. Taking a creative path that no other person on earth has taken. As the creamy oil paint is applied in thin layers, then more thickly, the outside world begins to evaporate around her. Sounds and feelings and tensions of the everyday world outside are barricaded as – like swimming – her mind plunges deeper and deeper to other things, the canvas seems bigger and all-consuming, and she slips, like a dying woman, into another world. Creativity emerges, the cares of the world submerge and vanish. She is twenty feet under water, her breathing becomes non-existent, a stress knot tightens across her shoulders, she catches a glimpse of herself in the studio mirror and she is pale and disorientated, but works on. Each brushstroke is a crucial decision. She is at war, but with whom? The elements… or herself? To darken one area makes another area appear lighter. To boldly paint pure white makes a black area appear blacker than black. A violet sky or yellow dusk? Grassy fields can, under certain light, appear blue, or yellow or purple. The underbelly of a rain cloud is never just grey; it can be crimson, blue, green sometimes. Each decision at thirty feet below the surface, becomes life or death. A week's work can be destroyed by a single hasty brushstroke. The world, with its rampant destruction of rain forests, the plight of the panda, the clubbing to death of baby seals, are now merely an existence existing somewhere else in the world. Disassociated and disjointed. Inspiration comes and goes; pleadingly teased from somewhere; it can vanish without trace like swallows in the autumn. But when it stays, even for a moment, she is in tune with the cosmos. She paints, unaware of time and space. She steps back, her head to one side, then the other. Did I actually paint that? she wonders. It was as if her blood and bone had been guided by an energy force greater than she. She blocks out a patch of brown and makes it white. She is working quickly, shifting the brushes with the dexterity of a surgeon, or a dentist. Forty feet down now. She can't remember when she last took a breath but she doesn't care; there are more important things to be doing than breathing. She wonders if she will be able to straighten up against the pain in her neck and shoulders. She remembers kind old men in straw hats and shorts, and delightful ladies who paint on Sunday afternoons remark that they find painting extremely relaxing, therapeutic even. 'Don't you find it relaxing?' they ask. No. How can you relax when you're forty feet down and gulping for inspiration? How can you be so suave and elegant when the responsibility of a God-given gift is on your shoulders, and making little of that gift flings it back thanklessly in His face? She grabs another, bigger brush and attacks the painting again and again, daubing, hatching, blocking in. Her eyes flick from one side of the canvas to another, sizing up, getting it right. More white. Her heart beats faster and she fears for her rising blood pressure. Some divine divine power is steering her and showing her the way. Her mind is totally submerged and she feels the hand of God upon her and –

– then the phone rings.

Will she let it ring? Curses for forgetting to unplug the damn thing. Could be an emergency.

She struggles to reach the surface. Drunk with frustration and disappointment, her mind is hauled through forty feet of inspiration, concentration, catapulting upwards, forcing itself to regain consciousness. She knows she must reach the surface and breathe earthly air before she can answer the phone.

From past experience she knows that eight out of ten phone calls will present a problem which, even when resolved, will occupy her thoughts for lost minutes, hours, the rest of the day. Her mind bids farewell to the dream state as she battles towards reality.

'Hello?' The sound of her own voice startles her; it sounds like someone else. For a second she doesn't hear the voice at the other end and when she does, she can't understand what they're talking about. 'Sorry, could you say that all again?' It turns out to be one of the eight.

She puts the phone back and slumps onto the sofa. A minor, easily resolved problem that the caller could have worked out for themselves has ended her day. She knows she won't return to that blissfully inspirational state now. The world, instead, has thunderously flooded back with all its doubts and fears and problems.

And yet, exhausted, she knows that she has created something of value, of worth, the only one of its kind, on the battlefield of the canvas. And she is happy.

FAMILY

I WORKED IN A PUBLISHING HOUSE for the last twenty-four years of my working life. I had toiled at a variety of other jobs before the publishing house; as a car salesman, (you were allowed to say 'man' in those days), a civil servant pushing pen and shuffling papers and wearing the bum out of my trousers every two months, and once I even had a cushy wee number as a security adviser to a national bank. When I took up the post in the publishers I honestly didn't think I would finish my working days there. If someone had told me I would be collecting my retirement watch and Waterford Crystal vase from the directors of Red River Publishing I would have told them to wise up and that there were at least another three or four careers left in me yet. That's just the sort of guy I am; always trying new things, taking risks, never really sure where I stand and never allowing myself the luxury of knowing a job inside out. Jack of all Trades, I suppose. That's why my longevity at Red River surprised me. But you never know what life's rich tapestry has in store for you, sure you don't?

For the twenty-four years I worked there, (God, almost a quarter of a century!) I lived in the same house, about ten miles away in the next small town, which was handy enough. I lived with my wife and two kids – a normal, everyday existence in a normal, everyday household. It meant that for twenty-four years I travelled that same uncluttered country road at 8.30 every morning and returned along it at about 5.45 that same evening, five days a week (with overtime one Saturday every four weeks), fifty-two weeks each year, for twenty-four years. I must be one of the only drivers in the country – if not the world – who can say that in all my time of driving to and from my place of employment I never once sat in a traffic jam.

I had just turned forty on that first spring morning in 1974 as I made my way excitedly to my new employment in my red Ford Escort, with a fresh white shirt and new tie, and Johnny Cash singing at San Quentin on my newly-installed 8-track. I felt like the bee's knees as I mimicked his Texan drawl, and it seemed to sum up my mood of light-heartedness and adventure on that first morning at 8.30. I knew the roads fairly well, and the stretch which I now travelled was only a few miles from my house, so I felt comfortable and at ease.

I got to know that road, every camber, every unrepaired pot hole, every bad bend, every straight which afforded me the opportunity to push that 1100 Ford engine to its full capacity and overtake the farmer as he indifferently bounced along in his tractor, or the granny in her Hillman Imp, oblivious to the world outside her windscreen.

If you travel any ten-mile stretch of road I'm sure you could pass anything between ten and a hundred similar-looking nondescript houses, with similar gardens and hedges and front doors and windows. It made me realise that whereas we all like to be different in some way, by us always trying to be different from everybody else, we are, in effect all doing the same thing and all looking alike – but that's another thought for another day. For some reason, even in those first few weeks of my taking up new employment, one house in particular attracted my attention. Well, it wasn't a house, really, it was a long squat bungalow, not a particularly attractive building, probably designed and built in the late sixties or early seventies by some trendy architect who earnestly believed that one day all homes will look like this. I, for one, am glad he was wrong. It had pebble-dash walls, and boasted enormous 'picture' windows with new-looking brown mahogany frames, and a huge inset front porch which, if bricked up could have formed the basis of another medium-sized room. The bungalow was set about twenty yards off the road, surrounded in ubiquitous shrubbery and manicured gardens. It was quite private and secluded; there was an extensive farm about a hundred yards further along the road, but other than that, the bungalow enjoyed uninterrupted views of the rolling countryside all around. Maybe it was because as you drove round a sweeping right hand bend, as you began to straighten, the bungalow was right in front of you, so that you could nearly see right into the living room, or lounge, as I'm sure it was called then.

For those first few months in 1974 the house was for sale. It lay vacant month after month, and I can remember feeling the frustration of the vendor, unable to clinch a quick sale; whether he was asking too much for it, or prospective buyers didn't like the idea of being so close to a farm, especially in the slurry season. Maybe I wasn't the only one who found the dwelling intolerably unappealing. Then one morning at the end of the summer a bold notice which read UNDER OFFER was attached to the For Sale sign. Things were looking up. I was glad. Then a few weeks later another sign declared that the bungalow was, at last, sold.

It was intriguing to watch the developments; those few weeks in which the bungalow lay in waiting for its new inhabitants, the grass on the front lawn became overgrown, even moss formed on the tiled roof which, in heavy rain would become saturated and drip and leave a stain down the front wall. A couple of times I saw a car in the driveway, sometimes somebody would be out looking at the roof, other times workmen would be shuffling about, pointing at drains, the septic tank, telegraph poles.

And just as, I believed, the bungalow was about to fall into an irreparable state, on a frosty morning in October a big blue removal van was parked proudly in the driveway. Two men – very business-like – were unloading boxes and bicycles and more boxes from the back, while a pretty young woman was busying herself between the back doors of the removal van and her new front door, while keeping one eye on the three children – two boys and one girl – in the garden. It reminded me of the flurry of excitement of two swallows, fresh from Africa, finding the site for their new nest in the eaves. One of the young boys was trying out his stabilised bicycle, the other boy was hanging out of a cherry tree at the bottom of the garden, while the little girl – the picture of her mother – was pushing her doll's pram about at the side of the house. The mother was concerned that her daughter didn't stray onto the unfamiliar road. I was sure that one of the men was her husband – the father – probably the one not wearing overalls. He was a lanky man, mid twenties, with a tie-dyed T shirt and longish hair and loons – just like every other man in the seventies, I suppose; a look that would cause cringing and embarrassment in years to come.

And that's what I saw of this new family on my five-second glimpse on that first morning as I drove past on my way to work. I found myself hoping that the family, still young and uncertain and unfamiliar, would be happy and safe in their new home, and that they would, ultimately, enjoy living there. Then my mind turned to trying to overtake the old grey-haired man with massive ears trundling along in his VW Beetle in front of me, and concerns about a deadline for a customer's order that day, and thoughts of the fledgling family disappeared.

Winter set in, and nothing much was done to the exterior of the bungalow for months on end. In fact, I hardly saw any of the family again until after the winter's hibernation, during which time the moss on the roof grew thicker and more saturated, the tar on the driveway began to crumble with the frost, and even bars of the fencing at the side of the road began to fall off, and were left unmended.

Some small effort of Christmas decorations eventually went up. A

Christmas tree with twinkling multi-coloured lights decorated the front window. It cheered me no end. And in the weeks after Christmas out came the shiny new bicycles, go-karts and Wendy house, a swing and a slide. A basketball net was erected above the garage door, but from that day to this I never as much as saw a ball being tossed at it.

And then one evening in late January, just when it's bright again at five o'clock when you're leaving work and your heart feels good, I passed at about 5.30 and all the children were out, admiring Dad's new car, shining and parked happily in front of the garage. A Volkswagen Passat. Green. The kids were bouncing in and out of the back seat, while the father was standing back, stroking his hair and admiring his purchase. His wife was trying out the passenger seat and laughing about something.

The school bus must have been late one morning and I saw the two boys in what I took as Primary School uniforms, patiently waiting with their mother at the front gate. She was holding their hands and staring apprehensively along the road. She glanced at my car as I passed, but that was all. There was no sign of the girl; she must be the youngest, I assumed. Probably still tucked up in her bed.

As the days lengthened and the cold strengthened the moss was at last scraped off the roof, and the stain on the wall cleaned. The fence at the side of the road was mended, and one morning a couple of tar-covered men were repairing the driveway; well, one was repairing the driveway while the other stood with a spade, watching on, and gulping tea from a mug the size of a saucepan.

The days had almost stretched to their summery fullness and there was Dad one morning with a brand new – well, at least it looked brand new to me – motorbike, gleaming beside the garage. He was down on one knee as if proposing, but instead he was polishing his new baby for all he was worth. I don't know the first thing about motorbikes – other than in a collision between a car and a motorcycle the biker usually comes off worse – so I can't enlighten you as to its make, CC, brake horse power or whatever they call it, but whatever it was, he was loving it. That evening he was still at it, but this time one of his boys – home from school and changed into his run-around duds – was sitting up on the seat, leaning forward, ducking and swerving and no doubt mimicking motorbike noises, pretending he was doing a hundred miles an hour. The little girl pushed her pram disinterestedly in the garden; talking, or maybe singing, to herself.

From the glimpses I got of the father he seemed a kind man. I never ever found out, or even got a clue as to what he worked at, but one thing was sure; he always seemed to make time for those children. He would pat his daughter's blond head, sit on the front steps, smoking a fag as the boys climbed over him, wrestling and tickling. As he washed his car the boys would be fervently helping him, in reality more of a hindrance than a help; probably dropping the sponge onto the tarmac, picking up small sharp stones and scraping the paintwork, or leaving big untouched areas of mud down the sides, but it didn't seem to bother him.

Occasionally I would see him getting into the car, probably going to work – wherever that was – lighting a cigarette and giving a wave to his wife at the door. Meanwhile she would hang endless basketfuls of washing on the clothesline at the back of the house, or rush from the house to the car in a shower of rain, bundling rapidly-growing children into the back seat, or arrive home in the evening with boxloads of groceries.

The only thing I ever saw the man do which was, I suppose, his way of making a statement to the passing world was, around September 1978, a flag, or bed sheet was pinned to the garage door with the words BOLAN LIVES ON sprayed, quite artistically, onto it.

At some time in the early eighties a second car appeared; a little

Panda, if my memory serves me right. They were now a two-car family. It was comforting to watch the slow but certain progress.

The boys became pimply-faced, straggle-haired adolescents, waiting begrudgingly for the bus, kicking at stones, hands in the pockets of their Secondary School uniforms, the name of the latest New Romantic band emblazoned on their rucksack schoolbags. Both boys acquired that gawky teenage appearance of testosterone-filled metamorphosis from child to man, where the developing bone structure simply doesn't match the skin and muscle around it. Gangly and self-conscious, sometimes in the evening they'd be kicking a ball to one another, both long past that sad point in every boy's life when the realisation that he will never be a professional footballer has well and truly sunk in.

I saw the girl's prams and dolls being demoted to the dark recesses of the garage, and short skirts, black eye makeup and multi-coloured hair take over.

The gleaming motorbike was brought out and shone up each spring. Maybe it wasn't the same bike as such (most likely wasn't) – they all looked the same to me – but it really did look good.

The big mahogany picture windows were replaced with white uPVC cottage-style types, and I thought they looked much better.

One Saturday in the middle of the summer I had to work later than usual so that I could get an important order finished and delivered to the customer, so I was passing the house at about seven-thirty or eight. Cars were parked bumper to bumper along the grass verge in such a long line that I had to slow right down in case a car came in the opposite direction. Fatalistically (as I usually am), I imagined the worst, fearing for the life of one of the family. Oh God, had something happened the wee girl? I shuddered. As I edged slowly past the parked cars – all good, clean motors, I must say – I heard Country and Western music. And even though, as is typical old C&W, it was mournful and miserable, at least my heart lifted when I looked across to see the family had organised a Cowboys and Indians barbecue. About thirty young people, couples, children, husbands and wives were gathered round a smoking half-barrel grill – all dressed as cowboys, Indians, undertakers, dance-hall girls, sheriffs – sipping American beers and laughing. They all looked fantastic; even the wee dog had a bandanna round its neck. The kids had erected a tepee at the bottom of the garden and were proceeding to shoot arrows through it. It all looked like great fun, and it put me in the notion of hosting my own barbie when I got home.

Over the years the Panda became a Fiesta, the single garage was extended into a double (probably to house the man's ever-growing zoo of motorbikes), the Christmas decorations grew bigger and more elaborate each year, eventually extending right across the front of the house with Santas, reindeers and snowmen. The boys became men, and the little blond girl became a bride.

I glimpsed her one morning in her wedding dress dashing out of the house followed by two bridesmaids and her mother. I could almost feel her mother holding back the tears. A gleaming wedding Limousine, decked out with ribbons and flowers, awaited her. She looked extraordinarily beautiful. For the first time in almost twenty years I could have gladly stopped my car and gone across and wished her all the best – but that would've been pointless. One of her brothers – I couldn't tell which – looked immaculate and proud in his suit and tie and sprig of white heather in his lapel, his hair now short and the teenage gawkiness gone.

One of the boys seemed to take more interest in motorbikes and engines and oily rags than the other, and I'd see him some evenings polishing and admiring the bike in the driveway or garage. He was all business helping his dad.

The daughter disappeared from the scene altogether having flown the nest and making her own home with her new husband God knows where. I missed seeing her.

The man's hair turned greyer, the woman lost her youthful slimness and became more rounded at the hips. She became less fastidious with her clothing; some mornings I'd see her hanging out the washing with her hair in a mess, wearing a dressing gown and socks and a cigarette in her mouth. But that's life.

On occasions I'd be driving along that road, most likely with the world's problems on my mind – scheming and planning – when a motorbike, with the rider crouched way down low, would pass me in a flash, or if he was coming the other way all I'd hear would be a short vvvrummm! as he whizzed by. Sometimes it actually scared me – the speed and the suddenness of it – and if I checked my face in the mirror after he passed I would be drained of all colour. I wondered, well, I assumed, that it was the man. Even had I known about motorbikes I still wouldn't have been able to identify it, or the rider, in the split second it took him to jet past me.

Over those years I realised one thing in particular; just how little time we, in this rainy, grey little island, spend outside in the open air. Our variable, four-seasons-in-one-day climate dictates that we gear our lifestyles to a life indoors, awaiting that one cloudless, fairly hot day each year when we all rush out and get dangerously sunburnt. We sneak out between showers to wash the car, cut the grass, brush the step, and so you could walk or drive around any built-up area and you might, if you're lucky, see one or two people… if any at all. It may sound as if I saw that little family every morning and every evening for twenty-four years, but in reality, if I caught a glimpse of them outside the house once every three or four, or maybe even six months, that would be the height of it.

Even so, slowly but surely, and depressingly so, it dawned on me that for a period of about six months, or maybe more, the bungalow fell sadly into its former state of disrepair. A black cloud seemed to hang ominously over it, probably because to me something was missing. I knew the family hadn't moved out – the two cars (now a VW Golf and a Peugeot 204) remained in the driveway, and to the best of my knowledge I hadn't seen a For Sale sign, but something had changed.

The grass grew long and unkempt again; at one time during the icy roads of winter some driver had obviously (or drunkenly) misjudged the bend and ploughed through the family's front fencing. The skid-marks which cut deep swathes through the lawn remained unrepaired, freezing, and covered in snow for weeks on end throughout January and February. To me, I sensed that the days of cowboy barbecues were a thing of the past.

The Golf was garaged and seemed to stay there, while the little blue Peugeot was always in one place or the other up the driveway, or not there at all. Even in the dark evenings the lights weren't on in the house. I felt as if I were a part of this anonymous family's misfortune, but not knowing what the misfortune was left me frustrated and worried. The home became a four-walled house, cold and inhospitable. Months of decay passed.

The first tentative warmth of spring came yet again; the Christmas decorations were long packed away, the frost and snow had turned to sharp cutting showers, and crows carried home-building twigs in their beaks to points high up in the trees. It was one such morning I saw him. There he was, in a wheelchair, sitting in the front porch. The once vibrant and vital father was now an invalid, pale and sickly-looking and dozing uncomfortably in the blindingly luminous sunshine of that morning. I shuddered, crushed, and a knot fisted in my stomach.

Each dry morning he sat there, eyes half closed, wrapped up well with a blanket and scarf, silent, looking into the far distance. Grey skin. I wanted to wave, toot the car horn, or something; anything to let him know that someone of whom he was unaware cared, and was concerned about him, and hoped he would make a full recovery from whatever had befallen him.

I saw that this once tall, energetic man had lost his stature, like all living things when nature tells them that life is drawing to a close.

Morning after morning I wondered what was going on in his head as he gazed towards the far hills. I missed him when he wasn't there; hoped to see him in the evenings but never did; even the act of sitting in a wheelchair doing nothing but gaze must have tired him out. When I didn't see him for weeks on end I feared the worst.

One morning he was sitting at the porch in the sun, glancing carelessly at a newspaper on his blanketed lap.

A week later he was reading a magazine with a bit more enthusiasm and interest, scanning the pages in detail.

Some time after that he was at the end of the driveway watching the cars go by, still sad and detached… thinking.

A month later he was quietly smoking a fag, and between drags sipping a mug of tea or coffee.

One evening on my way home from work I saw him, with a hint of a sun tan on his face and arms, clipping the front hedge.

Before the summer was out he was in the middle of the garden, still totally dependent on his wheelchair, pruning drooping wayward branches off the cherry tree.

On a warm September evening I glanced over to see him cradling a baby, with his wife and daughter – now a mother herself – chatting and laughing in the sunshine at the porch.

I set a date for my retirement. October the 16th. I couldn't believe I'd done – and enjoyed – twenty-four years in the same place, under the same roof, at the same desk.

I drove into work for the final morning on the sixteenth of October in my green Mondeo, not expecting to do much; just clear my desk and brief the new man who would be taking over from me, eat celebratory sticky buns and cake, maybe sip a glass of champagne supplied by Red River Publishing. I would collect my watch and Waterford Crystal vase after a hastily-prepared and stuttering speech, and generally try to thwart those rogue tears from filling my eyes as they do at the most inconvenient moments.

I rounded the corner at the bungalow for the last time; that right-hander which gave me a full view of the building, but which I could hardly now see because those bloody aforementioned tears had started early. He was there, at the end of the driveway, with the baby wrapped up and cuddled on his knees. He was smiling down and teasing the baby's mouth with his finger. I slowed as much as I could without attracting his attention. I slowed. And slowed. I wanted to drink in as much of these last few split seconds as I could.

He was stroking the baby's head now and smiling, the way he had done with his own daughter a quarter of a century before. I couldn't slow down unnoticed anymore and the decelerating engine made him look up. I looked him straight in the eye. He looked me straight in the eye. He looked different close up. Like a stranger. But he was a stranger. I gave the car horn a short, friendly toot and smiled. He smiled back, lifted his hand and gave a cheery wave. I waved as well... more like a thumbs up. I accelerated slowly away and with the corner of my eye I saw him return to amuse the baby, making a funny face.

I like to think he recognised me.

FIXING A RATTLE

THERE'S AN ANNOYING RATTLE IN MY CAR. Somewhere down near the driver's side rear wheel. When I turn the car to the right this thing which is causing the rattle sometimes rolls to the left, and when I turn to the left it rolls to the right. I've looked under the car but I just can't find it. I took the back seats out and carpets and everything to look for it but couldn't find it, and still it rattles. But it doesn't roll or rattle when the car is stopped so it's impossible to pinpoint where it's coming from unless the car is moving. Believe me it's really doing my head in. At one point on a long, winding journey I was ready for the madhouse. But then I thought, if I manage to find and remove this rattle, it would be no sooner fixed until another rattle would take its place. The original rattle is, in effect, stopping other rattles. So I'll not bother fixing this one.

ONE LAST GIG

JOHNNY MANN WAS WATCHING an afternoon cookery show in his bathrobe, wondering just how much of Jamie Oliver's saliva gets into his food when the doorbell rang.

'Mister Mann?'

'Yes, that's me,' said Johnny, 'but if you're sellin' anything I'm busy.' The man smiled. Usually people weren't just so frank.

'No, I'm not selling anything. The name's Gerry McNee and I hear y' used to play a bitta music in your day.' He looked at Johnny in anticipation, shuffling his feet and forcing another smile.

'Yea. Yea, I did, once, but not no more,' said Johnny, a bit fuller of face and greyer of temple since the last time he *played a bitta music* to an indifferent and inhospitable audience, thus resulting in his premature retirement from the pub, club and wedding scene all those years ago. Occasionally, some nights he would dream of gigging; of setting up his PA equipment piece by piece, of wondering with trepidation if the gig would go well in this strange place, but in each dream something would go wrong; nobody would turn up, the guitar had no strings, he would forget the words of a song…

'Too many late nights,' he said to the man at his door, dropping his eyes to the man's restless feet.

'I'm sorry to have bothered you then, Mister Mann—'

'Johnny.' He hated being called Mister Mann; it made him sound like a children's cartoon character.

'Sorry to have bothered you then, Johnny. It's just that you were recommended to me by two or three different people who had a great word for you... said you were a great entertainer and all that... '

'Is that so?' said Johnny, almost sadly. 'They must have been the only two or three people on planet Earth who liked what I did. Jeezus, with that amount of support I should've started my own fan club. Men or women?'

'Men.'

'Just my luck. At one time at the height of my fame I had ten women banging on my hotel room door – but I wouldn't let them out.'

Gerry McNee laughed. Johnny didn't. He couldn't recall a single memory of his thirty years gigging that was worth laughing at, never mind smiling. Yes, it'd had its moments, but if he laughed it was with cynicism. At drunk men talking crap and even drunker women losing all sense of decency. There comes a time in all of life's situations when you've had enough, when you have to finally stop forgiving, and Johnny's swansong had come about when his only memories of a once almost professional hobby were of passively smoking the blue nicotine of thousands of grotesque smokers, smug and thoughtless, leaving him with a permanently irritated throat and wondering if it was only a matter of time before the Big C formed a lump that he wouldn't be able to ignore. Of lugging speaker cabinets and amps, guitars, keyboards and a vast assortment of black-boxed equipment from van to stage and stage to van, up and down steps and stairs, nudging past pint-handed punters with an ill-disguised *scuse me, mate*, fifty times a night while warm, smoky sweat slid down his spine and face on a frosty Sunday at two in the morning. Of the endless requests for Country and Western, *keep 'er country!*, or worse still, Country and Irish. The Gambler. Coward of the County. Do y' know any of Daniel O'Donnell's early stuff? Garth Brooks, Kris Kristofferson, the Wee Man from Strabane; men who made a living from three chords, a vocal range of the same number of notes, and a miserable tale. He remembered with disgust the power struggle once a week, week after week between him on the stage and the obnoxious knucklehead trying to impress his girlfriend at the first table. The girl would usually appreciate the musician's set, but the jealous boyfriend didn't appreciate her admiring glances stage ward, so he would seethe and get all possessive to the point of getting up and making a loud remonstration of requesting Johnny to sing some obscure song from some obscure singer or band's obscure third album – a song that not another person in the world would have heard of, or even care to remember. 'No, sorry mate, I don't know it,' Johnny would offer in appeasement, feigning apology but wishing the asshole would slowly asphyxiate and die in front of him. The joker's eyes would widen in disbelief. 'You don't know it?' he'd shout, looking down to see if his girlfriend was amazed. 'You're not going to sit there and tell me y' don't know *Bring Down the Government* by *Betty and the Dolls*? Call yerself a musician? Ach, come on, yer *bounda* know it!' He would make a theatrical *I can't believe it* gesture and return to his seat, safe in the knowledge that he – a lowly bricklayer or car mechanic or fully-qualified asshole – knew a song that the singer (who was getting paid good money, by the way) didn't know. If Johnny remained diplomatic and professional and bided his time, eventually he would see the girl rolling her eyes and thinking what a twat I have for a boyfriend, and when the boyfriend would later go for a pee, glancing at the pathetic musician on his way out, she would invariably seize the opportunity and smile oh so coyly and seductively up at Johnny on stage. Wrapped in smugness, Johnny would make time during the next song to secretly smile back, knowing that his antagonist was probably at that minute obliviously preening himself in the bathroom mirror. He'd won that battle, and just for badness would steal flirting glances with the girl the rest of the evening. Oh! The psychology of it all! It was never a matter of learning thirty or forty songs and going out and simply playing them. In order to survive there were mind games, mental battles, wars of attrition, jealousies, struggles. Cerebral chess, Johnny called it. How to win hearts and minds. How do you win over an audience of lovers of Country and Irish? Sometimes it worked. You could fool some of the people… Sometimes, well… you went home drained and demoralised.

'We'd love you to have played at a charity night we're running in Tullyhappy…' Johnny didn't hear the remainder of the sentence. He was aware that Gerry McNee had continued on in his Sunday-school teacher-type patter, but two major factors had hijacked Johnny's mind and began to slap him about the face with austere clarity. Number one. Charity Night. At the mention of charity night Johnny's mind fought off flashbacks of nice, community-spirited people with their hearts in the right place serving flaky sausage rolls and greasy cocktail sausages and egg and onion sandwiches with a Biblical smile, a long-winded spokesman with a convivial speech, an old biddy with a lemon pleated skirt nervously accepting the over-sized cheque. Of stony-faced councillors with white hair and grey suits wiping sweat off their brows and talking drivel – anything to get themselves re-elected – while modern parents sipped fizzy water and talked about affairs of the Church of the Vacant Stare and nobody, but nobody in the slightest interested in the musician slogging his guts out in the corner. Number two. Tullyhappy. This jovial-sounding sleepy hamlet of three houses and a pub in Moyle – the least populated area in the British Isles, only slightly more deserted than the Shetland and Hebridean Islands – was, musically, the Irish equivalent to Nashville. It was *Smoky and the Bandit, Deliverance*, and the *Dukes of Hazzard* rolled into one. It was a three chord apocalypse, and Johnny couldn't help but smirk at the thought, and the dread of it, and be thankful he wasn't anywhere near it. Nor would he be casting his pearls before swine ever again.

'That's a pity,' said Johnny, 'but like I say I don't do it anymore; I'll leave it up to the young bucks who need the pocket money. My back started playin' me up in the end, as well.' But as he spoke, behind the excuses and the well thought-out justifications, he knew he was masking the real reason; when he got right down to it he was scared.

'Didn't you have a CD out an' all?' Gerry McNee insisted.

'Yea. Twelve easily forgotten, over-produced songs.' The man saw he was getting nowhere.

'Well, Mister Mann, (Johnny), I'll not take up any more of your time – sorry to have bothered you. I take it you got a quare sickener at some time.'

'You could say that.'

Gerry McNee stuck his hands deep into his coat pocket and braced himself against the fresh autumn air and started to make his way to his Renault Clio, where his wife had been thumbing through a magazine in the front seat.

'What charity are you running the event for, anyway,' Johnny asked, beginning to close his door and realising he'd probably come across as a bit acerbic and dispassionate.

'Meadowlands – the local children's hospice...' Standing uncomfortably barefoot on his doorstep Johnny glanced up at the sky as if searching for divine guidance, but as usual there was none, so he called after the man, 'Gerry... come in for a minute and we'll talk about it.'

'When you mention the hospice I'd love to help. I can't *not* help,' Johnny said. 'But Tully-bloody-happy? Of all places! It's the rootin' tootin' capital of the North. I don't do country... they'd hate me... they'd lynch me... I wouldn't get out alive!'

'Not atall not atall,' said Gerry McNee. 'The ones who advised me to get in touch with you said you'd be a breath of fresh air. Not everybody likes rinky-tink y'know.'

'Y' could've fooled me.' Johnny seemed always to have been the act who would be used as a guinea pig to find out if the local pigeon club or war veterans' association could do without Country for a night. The answer was usually a dismal no.

'It should be a great night…'

Johnny thought in his mind, 'I know exactly the sort of great night you're talking about,' but instead he said with his mouth, 'Y'know I don't think I'm as good as your friend says I am. I just use my guitar; no backing tapes or disks, no big band sound, no drum machine… warts and all.'

'Excellent!' Gerry McNee enthused. 'A bit of *real* music is what we need for a change. What d' y' think?' Johnny took a deep breath and sighed audibly. Still no guidance from above.

'Okay,' he agreed. 'What the hell… I'll do it. Call me a sucker.' In a way, Johnny was happy that he had accepted the offer. 'Did you ever try selling snow to Eskimos? You should try it some time – you'd make a fortune.' Gerry McNee threw his head back and laughed.

'I take it that's a yes?'

'On one condition: at the first request *for something by Garth Brooks* I'll unplug the guitar and I'm outta there!' They both laughed and shook hands.

Johnny needed coffee – lots of it. He slung a swig of Bush into his mug. The coolly persuasive man with a pleasant approach was no sooner round the corner, with his wife waving thankfully through her suede mittens when Johnny regretted having allowed himself to be hauled from his cosy retirement and back into a world of God knows what. He had to admit it: he was a sucker for a gig. The boy who couldn't say no. Eejit. And yet he knew he was too old for all this hassle. He had called his retirement and now he wished he'd stuck to his resolution. Life had moved on. He had felt the pain of age when his son came home one day with his first heavy metal CD, (he had called it heavy *ass* metal) and Johnny, trying to be young and cool, had asked him what was on the *flipside*. And he recognised the teenage raised eyebrows of his daughter planning her first trip to France when he had asked her what she was going to do *on the Continent*. 'Where?' she asked. 'Is Continent the old name for Europe?' He remembered a million years ago when, on a Saturday evening after a shopping expedition by bus to Belfast with his mum and dad he would parade in his new Cardinal Red sandals, or his first long trousers, or a new Sloppy Joe, and his grandmother would rub her hands and go, 'Ah boys a dear, aren't you the quare smasher!'

He – now safely past his mid-life crisis and living to tell the story – with his mortgage under control and having forgotten every song he had ever played week after week for twenty years – had agreed to perform once again. But times, and people had changed. He would be playing to a new generation of unsmiling, overweight drab teenagers who watch old black-and-white footage of The Beatles and wonder what all the fuss was about. Westlife are better, they declare. Gareth Gates can write better songs than Paul McCartney any day. He'd be performing to a cynical pack of proles who are being taught in school that Hitler wasn't such a bad guy after all – just a wee bit misguided. Poor old Adolf's heart was in the right place. This new slick designer generation of over-confident mummies' boys can communicate only with a mobile phone in their ear, or by utilisation of a complex system of grunts and mumbles that only their immediate peers seem to understand. The more he thought of what he'd let himself in for he knew – he just knew – that he was going to bomb like no other act in the history of pub singers had bombed before.

He'd long since sold his wee blue van, so he struggled to fit all his old PA equipment into the car, but he eventually got it. He'd advertised his PA in the Telegraph for a couple of nights a few years ago but there wasn't a single enquiry, so it had lain in the corner of the garage getting more damp and mouldy by the year. He'd scribbled a list of everything he'd possibly need to get him through the night, like a pair of pliers in case he needed to change a string, and a small bar towel for his face in case he broke sweat. On second thoughts, he envisaged doing a lot of sweating before the night was through. And headache tablets.

It was a Saturday evening as he drove northward through the bumpy Glens of Antrim and every radio station he tuned into was thumping out its pre-club, mindless bmmp bmmp bmmp bmmp, firing up the young impressionable minds for a night of asinine garbage to dance to. He mused, even managed a smile, when he decided that if the greatest musical genius of all time – Wolfgang Amadeus Mozart – could hear the inane, worthless musical crap of the twenty-first century , he would probably perform slow, bodily revolutions in his final resting place. He smiled to himself again, but it was a smile that cloaked his trepidation.

A Corsa full of baseball-capped pimples pulled alongside him at traffic lights. An unearthly purple fluorescent glow emanated from the chassis, while little silly blue lights twinkled on the bonnet. The rise of the chav. From inside came a resonating bmmp bmmp bmmp bmmp and when the tinted passenger's window slowly wound down, a few beer cans and the remains of a Chinese carryout were tossed onto the footpath, landing like a little dead white rabbit.

The owner of the pub – it was easily enough found – had a firm handshake and showed him the 'stage' – a small dark corner in a small dark room. The landlord, almost apologetically, kept saying that the night's entertainment was *all for a good cause*. Johnny took no comfort in this; the Provisional IRA would probably say the same thing. He was an intense wee man; as if running a one-horse-town country pub put too great a weight on his shoulders, and, like every other person in the world with bad breath, he spoke up close – too close. Sometimes Johnny gagged and went about removing the jammed-in gear from his car.

Now he was getting plain nervous, and he felt it right down to his gurgling colon. When Johnny was anxious about something he tended to trip on his tongue, and gibber, as if trying to squeeze twenty thoughts into one sentence simultaneously, and he detested himself for it. Most times, in his rush to get something said, he would join two or three sentences together as one, and out came an incoherent concoction of nonsense. It had sounded okay and rational and perfectly formed in his head, but when he thought about what he had been bumbling about later it made him cringe with embarrassment.

There was a middle-aged man with a cowboy shirt and black leather waistcoat carrying a Yamaha keyboard of some description under one arm and a mic stand under the other, making his way out of the bar and towards his car, which had been parked as close to the pub door as possible with the boot open. With his drowned-rat moustache and Cuban heels he looked like something straight out of the set of *The Good, the Bad, and the Ugly*. Starring as the Ugly, of course. The landlord, garrulous as ever, explained that *Big Clint* had been playing at a wedding the night before and was just here to collect his gear, although he may call back for a beer later and support the charity event. A *wedding*? In *here*? Finding this implausible and yet amusing Johnny nodded at Big Clint, who growled something in return, maybe peeved that some new face was encroaching on his territory. Big Clint was the bossman of his Ponderosa and no greenhorn was gonna make him no trouble. Johnny's nerves left him, but he so wanted to speak, to break the ice, to say something witty but friendly, like. One side of his tormented brain was preparing to ask Big Clint, 'Were you playing here last night?' while on the tip of his tongue the other half was planning, 'Did it go well last night?' But with his mind fumbling as it did in such instances he opened his mouth and heard himself say with a mouth that seemed to belong to someone else, 'Did you play well last night?' Big Clint glowered down at Johnny.

'What was that?'

Johnny coughed and smiled and pretended that it wasn't he who had spoken in the first place. He walked away, letting the situation hang in mid air like a fart in an elevator; hoping it would just blow away.

He puffed as he lifted the speaker cabinet onto its stand. That used to be easy, he thought. Then he had to sit down and catch his breath. The encounter with Big Clint reminded him, with wincing, of the time he went with a friend for a day's racing with the geegees at Royal Ascot. As he stood studying his race card at an otherwise deserted paddock he became aware of a diminutive female figure to his right, quietly checking the form as well. Through the corner of his eye – or maybe it was instinct – he could discern that the powder-blue clad old lady was examining the horses with an expert eye. Not wanting to appear aloof he turned to say good morning, or something, and found himself eye to eye with the Queen Mother herself, in all her royal refinery. Her bodyguards were chatting to one another a little way off, oblivious to the terror that was going on in Johnny's head. In a flurry of alarm Johnny realised that if he opened his mouth with his Ulster accent the bodyguards would be on him like bears on a beagle. Before he could say Buckingham Palace the Queen Mother curled her gentle lips into the most disarming smile. He *had* to say something – *now*. He couldn't just stand there all day with that blank, imbecilic stare. But what? In the time it took the lovely old lady to smile he had worked out that he couldn't just utter a cold, 'Hello'. That would be too harsh. He had to address her as something, but what in the name of goodness was her name? Queen Mother? No, his mind raced, you can't say, 'Hello, Queen Mother'. She's not the Queen so you can't call her Queen anything. Time was running out, he had precisely one nano second to think of how to address her when his mouth, which so frequently took on a life of its own, opened again and he heard to his dismay, 'Hello... Mother'. And the old lady continued to smile, probably out of pity than anything else. Johnny had then sauntered over to the beer tent, biting his knuckles and squirming.

Big Clint's rusty diesel Citroen Estate rattled off into the night, and Johnny was alone.

Things that Johnny at one time could have done blindfolded with the lights out – like knowing where each cable and lead fitted into the spaghetti junction behind the amp, tuning his guitar, doing a sound check – were now impossibly arduous and difficult and took him twice the time. His voice quaked as he did his one, two, one two sound check, and yes, even now, after all these years' absence some big-brained twit at the bar shouted, 'The next number's three!' the same as they had done since the first microphone was invented. Some irritating things just wouldn't go away, like the beer belly he had installed in his thirties and which now rolled like a pig's backside in front of him.

Punters started to arrive, politely and quietly taking their places, sometimes smiling at the new face in the corner. 'Things are bad when y' have to come to a kip like this,' someone quipped. But at least they weren't hostile – yet.

Johnny propped his battered old Gibson acoustic against his bar stool and ambled over to the bar for a shandy. He caught a glimpse of himself in the mirror behind the bar, his face wedged between the whiskey and vodka bottles on the shelf. He'd caught that look so many times before; as a teenager wondering if he was going to get off with some unsuspecting female that night (remembering his father's wisecrack advice that if you're not in bed by ten o'clock just go on home to your wife), as a drunken effigy wondering how he was going to get home, but most times it was as an anxious entertainer sizing up his audience and wondering how the gig was going to turn out. He thought he looked okay tonight, if he remembered to hold his belly in. He'd gone for an understated, moody, Man in Black look. He'd had a blue shirt in his hands as he stood at the wardrobe earlier on, but then remembered that wearing blue had the power to actually make him feel queasy and unhappy, and his face to look paler than usual. The black jacket with a Beatle collar looked good – a sort of uncanny cross between Sting and Johnny Cash.

Soon, surprisingly, the room began to fill up. More welcoming smiles from well-dressed, casual, educated sort of people. A sociable atmosphere seeped into the room and seemed to lighten the darkness. An entertainer can sense an atmosphere, whether friendly or hostile, a mile off. His sensors are as much tuned in to fluctuations in the social mood as a great white shark is to a panic-stricken swimmer on the horizon. A quiz was hastily organised and a couple of good-natured party games had everybody laughing and bantering. The proverbial sausage rolls were produced by the landlady and soon only white plates littered with crumbling crusts remained. Johnny watched as one man scoffed his food; opening his mouth disgustingly far wider than was required for the scrawny bite he was taking. Johnny was sure he caught glimpses of the man's larynx, and it made his stomach churn. He watched a woman nibble like a gerbil her curly ham-and-cheese sandwich as if she were eating a cherry and trying to separate the pip from the fruit using only her front teeth. He was glad to see abundant amounts of drink being imbibed, and soon ties were loosened, jokes got dirtier, voices got louder. A strong arm contest was announced – between two women – one who looked like Meat Loaf and the other was the spit of Alice Cooper. It was like a Battle of the Bands, and it drew a crowd of cheering men and women round the table, reminiscent of the Russian Roulette scene from *The Deerhunter*.

As Johnny took to the stage the noise in the place was cacophonous. Gerry McNee came over, unsteady on his feet, shook hands for the twentieth time and asked Johnny if everything was cool.

'As well as can be expected, under the circumstances,' Johnny said, trying to sound uplifted.

'Don't worry, you'll be one hundred percent. They're all mental.' He trundled off excitedly to check the answers of the quiz.

There was no decrease in the noise level as Johnny at last plumped himself down on his bar stool and adjusted the mic comfortably in front of his mouth. He was terrified, almost to the point of incontinence, yet his head told him there was no need to be; he wasn't aiming to change the world any longer and not one single solitary person was looking in his direction. To them he was just another one-man band on a Saturday night. A one-man band who will croon through a cheap PA all the usual numbers to please a crowd and who will be swiftly forgotten by first thing on Sunday morning. They were laughing and drinking and flirting and enjoying themselves. He was now afraid that he, Johnny Mann – washed up failure from another era – was going to spoil all that. He looked out from under the two red spotlights at the young, and middle-aged, and elderly gathering and wondered how in God's name he was going to please everybody. Then one of his old homespun philosophies rang in his head: *try to please everybody and you end up pleasing no-one.* That was one of his favourites. *Don't throw the old one out until you're sure the new one's working. Before you make your attack prepare your escape. When in doubt – buy a loaf.* But try as he may, he got no comfort from his mental wanderings.

Just as he was about to address himself to his audience for the night Gerry McNee came up on stage and asked to borrow the mic. Johnny hated anyone else talking through his mic, but for tonight he allowed it anyway. If a man or woman who borrows the mic has a throat infection or some other disease of the oesophagus the entertainer will have contracted the same complaint by the next morning, so spending the rest of the week sucking throat lozenges and gargling with TCP.

'A bitta hush!' he shouted, so loudly that the speaker behind him blared out nothing but ear-piercing feedback. Johnny's heart thumped louder than the boom from the speakers. 'A BITTA HUSH! PLEEEEEZE!' Slowly and reluctantly the noise abated. 'We've had a great bitta banter so far tonight so we have, and now will y' all put yer hands together for some real music. Please give a big Tullyhappy welcome to Mister Johnny Mann!' There was whistling and applause, but they didn't know Johnny and what he sounded like and the sort of stuff he did, so what were they applauding for?

Johnny was glad of the crowd at the bar who partied on as if he wasn't there, and the football supporters who banged and cursed at the gaming machines in the corner. Around his feet a few tables went respectfully quiet in anticipation. Johnny let the first finger-picked notes of Elton John's *Your Song* fill the air. C F G F; a mellow intro, but then he'd always billed himself as the Maestro of Mellow. He could feel the audience wait longingly for the drum machine to come in, and the heavy plonking of a country bass, overlaid with twangy steel guitar. But there was none, and he sensed their disappointment. Johnny felt himself bombing on his first song. He could've easily vomited instead of singing. Why had he let himself be talked into this torment? And just like at other times when his mouth seemed to take on an existence of its own, he took a deep breath, closed his eyes, and allowed the song to flow.

A woman in a swarm of raucous men shouted, 'Sssssh! Oh God I love that song!' The men turned in their seats. The woman – with dangerously exposed cleavage, but if you have it, flaunt it – began singing along with Johnny. It humoured the men for a couple of seconds – the woman's cleavage that is, not Johnny's song – and soon they returned to arguing that even though Arsenal were at present dominating the domestic football scene they would never be looked upon as one of the *truly great teams of all time*, like the Manchester United of the sixties and nineties and the Liverpool of the seventies. As Johnny slowed the ballad to a close the woman applauded frenetically.

Two men clapped uninterestedly, the barman clapped loudly and whistled to try and get things warmed up. Johnny said, 'Thanks. Thanks a lot. It's lovely to be here tonight folks... I hope you raise plenty of money for the hospice... it's a good cause.' Some shut up to listen and applauded politely and quietly. Johnny went on, 'As you can see, it's just me and my old gee-tar, warts, mistakes and all, but I hope you enjoy the rest of my set for the evening. Sing along if you feel moved. So, without further eloquence...' and he tinkled into what he named a *classic song by The Eagles*. At the chorus of *Peaceful Easy Feeling* Johnny caught glimpses of men and women mouthing along with him. That was always a good sign. One drummed on the beer-lathered table with a table mat, while three young hens at the next table put their arms round each other and swayed to the melody. Johnny let the guitar solo slow down and then speed up, like waves on an ocean, contrasting with thoughts of sleeping in the desert tonight. On the last note of the song two young guys who looked as if they may be in a band themselves turned from their girlfriends and applauded, holding their hands high and clapping like a substituted footballer acknowledging his supporters. 'Thanks,' said Johnny. 'Thank you.' Without stopping to tune he went straight into '...the Simon and Garfunkel classic, *Mrs Robinson*.' He played it harder and faster than Paul and Art, grittily spitting out cup cakes and Jesus loves you, Mrs Robinson, and the large-cupped lady was now up and bouncing about and the men keeping time with the beat and at the four sharp chords at the end of the song... a miracle happened: everybody, but *everybody* in that room applauded wildly, cheered, whistled, and called for more.

Johnny's confidence soared through the roof. Sweat seeped down the back of his black shirt and soaked his underpants, saturated his chest, drenched his hair, stung his eyes, trickled off his nose... but he played on, oblivious to any minor discomfort. He sang the whole ten minutes' worth of *American Pie*, dazzled his adoring audience with the exotic *Paint it Black*, followed closely by *Sunny Afternoon, Horse With No Name, Tambourine Man* – even Pink Floyd's *Wish You Were Here* – and still they yelled for more. Johnny Mann could do no wrong. Young people said hey, this guy's good, man. Fortysomethings declared, God I haven't heard that song in a quare while, and when he sang *Ride a White Swan* – the song that had started it all off for him in the beginning – the woman who looked like Meat Loaf screamed in his face, 'Marc Boreland was the greatest!'

Through the mists of adoration, nicotine and triumph, Johnny looked up to see a huge, shadowy figure emerge. It was Big Clint. It just had to be. Sent to spoil his night. This was going to be the Phantom at the Feast. Johnny had just finished Bowie's *Starman* and Big Clint asked, 'What about something by Garth Brooks?'

'Who?' said Johnny, delaying.

'Garth Brooks. You're bounda know *If The Morra Never Comes*.'

'Sorry big lad,' said Johnny, '…don't do any of his stuff.'

'Why not?' growled Big Clint.

'Cos he doesn't do any of mine…' That flummoxed Big Clint. He scratched his chin and rubbed the back of his leather neck.

'Fair enough,' he conceded. 'Y' have a point there.' Big Clint returned to his misty corner and his pint to work it out.

Pints of gratis shandy now stood guard on his amp. Calls of anything by Van the Man, T.Rex, Donovan, Buddy Holly, Elvis roared around the room and were miraculously all part and parcel of Johnny's long-established set list, and he performed them all with relish. At one point an astoundingly fine-looking woman nudged her way through the crowd, introduced herself as Molly and shouted into Johnny's ear that he was the best act she'd ever seen. 'Why are you not world famous?' She shook his hand, turned away, and was suddenly swallowed up by the heaving multitude. No small praise, eh? The small dance floor filled with revellers who sighed loudly when Johnny announced that *Whiskey In The Jar* would be his last song. Where had the night gone? *Temperas fugit* when you're enjoying yourself. Men stomped the floor. More! More! More! More! So Johnny strung on his guitar again and joined five Beatles' songs together, *All My Loving, I Want to Hold Your Hand, Strawberry Fields, Eleanor Rigby*, ending with the Na Na Na Nanana Na chorus at the end of *Hey Jude* with everyone swaying with upheld cigarette lighters, smooching, hugging and singing along like a New Year's Eve party.

'Goodnight, and thanks for a great night's repartee,' shouted Johnny, blind with sweat and exhilaration. It was his finest hour. Alice Cooper fought her way to the stage and hugged Johnny. 'That was the best night we've had in here for a long time!' Big Clint came out of the mist and shook Johnny's hand and said, solemnly and simply, 'Talented guy.' Gerry McNee, now almost unconscious, bounced onto the stage, grabbed the mic and shouted, 'Put yer hands t'g'er forr Mishter Jonathon Mann! You've all heard of Van the Man, but this here is *thee* Mann!' When the cheers died down and the joyful crowd gave up calling for an encore, he added, 'Now foksh, please be upstanding forr the National Antrim…'

Gerry McNee stopped Johnny later in the hallway as he struggled with his guitar case and amp through twenty inebriate sycophants, all begging for his return some time in the very near future. They were joined by Gerry's wife (who, it turned out, was the secretary of the Friends of the Hospice) and another organiser, a serious, sober man with a cheque book in his hand. Seeing that Gerry was incapable of coherent speech, the man told Johnny that everybody had loved his music and had had a great night. It was great to hear some real music for a change. He asked Johnny how much they owed him. 'Nothing,' Johnny said. 'Give it to the hospice.'

By
JOHN CONNERY
and available from Red Hill

The Insular People
a collection of Irish yarns
£6.99

Under a Blackthorn Bush
another collection of Irish short stories
£6.99

FREE POST AND PACKAGING IN IRELAND
Overseas customers allow £2.00 per paperback

BY POST: Red Hill Publications
P.O. Box 557 Craigavon BT64 9AG

BY EMAIL: red.hill7@btinternet.com

Cheques only (payable to Red Hill)

Allow 28 days for delivery

When placing your order please mention if you would like additional
information about John Connery's writing or art.